SARVET'S
Wanderyar

Also by J.M. Ney-Grimm

Livli's Gift

Troll-magic

The Troll's Belt

Rainbow's Lodestone

Star-drake

Perilous Chance

SARVET'S
Wanderyar

A tale of the mountain-folk
of the Fiordhammars

by J.M. Ney-Grimm

Wild
Unicorn

Sarvet's Wanderyar
may also be found in the collection
Sarvet & Livli
along with its sequel
Livli's Gift

ISBN-13: 978-0615743097
ISBN-10: 0615743099

Designed by JMNG

Cover art by Kay Nielsen

To Wendy,
for her enthusiasm and encouragement

SARVET'S
Wanderyar

*T*ense and furious, Sarvet shook her mother's angry grip from her forearm. "I'll petition the lodge-meet for filial severance," she snapped, and then wished she'd swallowed the words, so hateful, too hateful to speak. And yet she'd spoken them.

The breeze swirling on the mountain slope picked up, nudging the springy branches of the three great pines at Sarvet's back and purring among their needles. Their scent infused the moving air.

Paiam's narrowed eyes widened an instant – in hurt? – flicked up to encompass the swaying tree tops behind her daughter, then went flat.

"You dare!" she breathed. "You're *my* daughter. Mine alone. And I'll see to it that you and every other mother in the lodge knows it too. You'll stay under my aegis till you're grown, young sister, even if I must declare you careless and remiss to do it!"

Oh!

Sarvet only thought she'd been mad before. "You never wanted me!" she accused.

Was it true? Or was she just aiming for Paiam's greatest vulnerability, aiming to hurt? Because under her own rage lay . . . desperation. Something needed to change. She just didn't know what, didn't know how. And didn't want to be facing it right now, facing her mother right now. It was Other-joy, and she wanted joy. For just a little longer. How had this day of celebration gone so wrong?

She'd woken to the pleasant consciousness that the morning of a fete-day brings. No chopping cabbage, digging potatoes, or long hours at the spinning wheel awaited her. The preparations for Other-joy were wholly different from normal chores, and this year the calling ritual would include three linking ceremonies!

She remembered smiling with anticipation, starting to push herself upright, then changing her mind to snuggle her cheek more deeply into her pillows. Light from the oil lanterns in the hallway was seeping through the chinks around her bednook shutters – Sister Teraisa must already be up – and Sarvet wanted to get up too. But not just yet. Her sheets were so soft, her blankets cozy, and the fur coverlet warm. She wriggled her toes in their bedsocks, ignoring the constraint in her right foot. There was something special to the first beginning of a day, all its promise ahead. She would savor it . . . and avoid a little longer the chilly moment when she doffed her nightcap and gown in order to dress.

She closed her eyes again and huddled her shoulders more securely under the bedclothes. Mmm. Because she was toasty from the neck down, the unheated air inside her bednook felt soft, refreshing even, on her cheek. *If only I could store warmth away like I store my sweaters on a shelf.* She would be shivering later, outdoors in the snow and the dark. Winter garb could do only so much. *If I could awake to Lodge-day instead of Other-joy this morning, would I?* She loved the clash of Other-joy's cold austerities with its equally warm and rich moments. But Other-joy was . . . complicated. Lodge-day was just fun. She'd spent it with her friend Amara last summer.

They'd greeted the men of Tukeva-lodge with traditional tossed thistle-silk streamers – a shower of crimson, gold, purple, amber, and blue pelted at the visitors as they approached the mother-lodge. Amara's father was a bear of a man, big and round and laughing, with a pillow of a beard. His hello hugs swooped Amara, Amara's mother Iteydet, Amara's aunt Enna, and Sarvet off their feet. His arms felt like tree limbs. Flexible ones. Only after his enthusiastic civility did Feljas gaze in puzzlement at Sarvet's face.

"But little Hilla never grew from belt high to chest high since Nerich!"

Amara broke into giggles. "Hilla's picnicking with her best friend, mapah! This is *my* best friend, of course. Sarvet."

"Then you'll excuse a mapah's zeal, little sister, won't you? I thought you were mine!" His eyes twinkled.

Sarvet found herself giggling along with Amara. "Of course," she answered. And knew a moment's wistfulness. *I wish he* were *my mapah.* But Ivvar would never visit Kaunis-lodge, even on the greater fete-days like Other-joy.

Feljas was more like a wixting-brother than a father. He claimed the very tip of the valley-rock for their picnic blanket, teased Enna unmercifully about the damage her long eyelashes would do to the hearts of unlinked brothers, juggled their luncheon pears in fancy patterns before passing them to each sister for eating, dropped kisses on Iteydet's cheek every fifth sentence, and pulled a sack of luxurious dried cherries from his capacious pocket for dessert. Then he fell asleep under Sarvet's amazed gaze.

Her expression must have conveyed her astonishment, because Iteydet ventured a laughing explanation. "He's always like this. Never stops until he *really* stops. In sleep. If I had to live with him day-in and day-out, like a sister, he'd wear on me."

But Hammarleeding women didn't live with their men. Sarvet had heard rumors that the Silmarish lowlanders did. Here in the mountains, sisters lived with sisters in the mother-lodges. And brothers lived with brothers in the father-lodges. As was proper.

Iteydet continued: "He'll wake again soon. And I'll be glad of it. It's not a proper fete-day without Feljas' jokes!"

He did wake. And proposed a game of tag combined with rolling down the mountain slope. Enna refused, but the sisters occupying three blankets near theirs were persuaded to join the fun, even including the normally staid Teraisa. Sarvet surprised herself when she abandoned keeping Enna company mere moments after her own plaintive refusal. Her limp was no disadvantage when rolling, not running, was the mode of movement.

The whole day had been like that: merry and easy and . . . loving. *Would* she trade Other-joy for Lodge-day? Yes! Well . . . maybe. Sarvet ducked her head down under the covers. No. *Other-joy is special.*

"Sarvet! Sarvet!"

The bright, excited voice of her friend Brionne sounded abruptly beside her bednook, followed immediately by the banging open of the foot shutter and Brionne herself bouncing in on the mattress. "Wake up! How can you still be sleeping? It's Other-joy!" Brionne's face was flushed and her eyes sparkled, but she was still in her nightclothes, for all her eagerness.

Sarvet clutched at the coverlet which Brionne's vigor had disarranged. The hall air was cold! "Stop," she protested half-heartedly. "Of course I wasn't asleep. Haven't you ever heard of a slow start to a day?" She hid a grin behind her hand, feigning a yawn.

"Arve!" Brionne's use of the old sweet-name was an unusual slip. She knew Sarvet was jealous of Amara (a year older than them both) and stretching away from childish things. Brionne must have believed the fake yawn.

"Girls!" Sister Teraisa's voice came low, but chiding. "Take it downstairs. Your neighbors are dreaming. Not everyone chooses to rise this early!"

Brionne pouted and lost some of her sparkle, but Sarvet couldn't resist giving her a reproving glance. *She* hadn't been the noisy one.

"I'm sorry, Sister Teraisa." Brionne was subdued, her surreptitious glance to her friend reproachful.

The Sister wasn't appeased, but she just shook her head, touched last finger to lip, and hurried away.

"Are you really going to stay here snoozing?" whispered Brionne. "If we attend first-calling, we'll get dried hoolinberries after. Come on, Sarvet, do get up!"

Sarvet relented. "I *am* up. But these covers stay put while you sit between me and the clothes in my cupboard. I'll move . . . when you do."

Brionne giggled, pulled a face, and slid out into the sleep-hall. Sarvet followed, wincing as her lame foot took her weight. It was always a little stiff right out of bed, even when she iced it in a bucket of snow before retiring. Of course, if she skipped the nightly icing, she couldn't walk at all until after Sister Evaia massaged the tightened tendons.

She rummaged through the shelf under her bednook, shivering, and pulled out her thickest wool stockings, felted boots, thistle-silk under garments, and her best sweater-tunic and hood in festive red. Brionne was ready first, as usual, garbed in her favorite forest green. Sarvet studied her friend. Her shiny, syrup-brown hair was so pretty. *I wish my hair were shiny instead of wooly.* But it wasn't. And . . . *who cares? It's Other-joy!*

Brionne searched the black sky through the clerestory windows above the bednooks for signs of dawn – none. She turned her head and smiled at Sarvet. "Ready?"

Sarvet nodded and pulled her hood over her ears. She was used to being slower. She knew her friends never thought about this difference anymore. But her palsied hip and twisted foot made the simplest tasks, even dressing, take longer. And she wished . . . the healing-call last year had worked instead of making things worse. *I won't think about that now. It's Other-joy, and I'm going to have fun!* She returned Brionne's smile, closed the cupboard door, and straightened.

The corridor was just wide enough for them to walk side by side. Brionne went slowly, not so that Sarvet – limping – could keep up, but because she knew Sister Teraisa would scold them for thumping, if they hurried. At least half the bednooks lining the passage on both sides still sheltered dreamers. First-calling was an optional rite on Other-joy, and many of the sisters of Kaunis-lodge skipped its rigors.

Snow-washing the face and hands outside in the ritual of detachment followed by searching one's heart for deep wishes in the darkness of the unlit calling-hall held little appeal for many. But Sarvet found the cold, clear purity of it exhilarating, especially compared to the close, hot, tangled asceticism practiced by her mother. *But I won't think of that either.*

And she didn't. The bones of her hands ached with cold when she returned them to their mittens, and the skin of her face felt numb after its bath in the snow, but the stars overhead – pulsing like remote fire-beacons – seemed to herald newness, hope, and adventure. The Holy Caller's voice (praying Divine Sias for oneness of being, knowing where self ended and other began, and fluidity in engagement) sounded joyous and full of life.

I love this.

Back indoors, sitting on a bench in the calling-hall, she wondered what her heart-deep wishes for this year might be. *I hoped for healing last year.* And that was a mistake. *I wish I could have a wanderyar, like the boys in their father-lodges.* Why couldn't girls travel from mother-lodge to mother-lodge for a year? *I want wider horizons too! That was why I wished for healing.*

She spared a glance for Brionne, beside her, and was surprised to see a tear quivering on her eyelash. What did her friend want so passionately that it inspired grief? *I thought she was happy.* She always seemed so bubbly and energetic and content.

Later, nearer dawn, breaking their fast in the refecting-hall, Brionne was all blushing laughter. Had

Sarvet really seen that tear? Her friend asked: "Can you imagine being a novitiate today?"

No, she couldn't.

"We will be, one day, you know."

"Not everyone choses the linking sacrament, Bri."

"So. Will you refuse? If Sister Valitte selects you?" Brionne directed a searching glance at her, then looked down.

"My mother did." Sarvet felt her face heating.

"Not her first time. You wouldn't be here, if she had." Brionne's smile grew serious. "Besides, don't you want to? It's supposed to be . . . nice."

"I don't know. I suppose I thought this" – she gestured at her leg – "meant I wouldn't be selected. I know my mother would prefer it that way." Sarvet shifted uncomfortably. Talk of brothers and linking and masculinity made her uneasy, but it was hard to avoid it on Other-joy. Especially once one was fifteen. She and Brionne would be meeting with Sister Kilti regularly soon, preparing for their own linking. It was rare that a sister under nineteen was chosen, but the women of the Kaunis-lodge liked every girl to be thoroughly ready.

"But . . . a birth injury couldn't be passed to your child!" Brionne looked startled. "You're not *vayatynt*, Arve!" The sweet-name again.

"No, but . . ." She didn't want to talk about her mother. Not today. And her mother was all tangled in this, although even she didn't understand how. "Bri, I haven't passed through my first blood yet." Another thing she was slow at. Both Brionne and Amara had reached that threshold before her. "I wish . . ."

Someone tapped her on the shoulder. "Sarvet! Brionne! Happy Other-joy!" Amara was glowing. The blue of her festival sweater-tunic and skirt always brought out the brilliance of her equally blue eyes, the richness of her smooth, chestnut curls. And her interruption was timely. The right words – *shun it*, the right *thoughts* – to get Bri onto another subject hadn't even begun to surface.

Amara walked around the end of the table to sit across from them. She looked enviously at their plates. The hoolinberries had been distributed to all the first-callers, but not yet eaten. "You lucky snow-pigs! Sister Tamma was generous!"

"You could have had some too, if you'd been willing to leave your dreams earlier," Brionne countered.

Amara tossed her head. "I needed my beauty sleep. Besides, I was up late." She snickered.

Sarvet felt her forehead wrinkling. Up late? Why?

"Sister Kilti remembered after all the oil lanterns were doused that I'd been ill the day she talked with the new witnesses about the secret rites." Of course Amara had to rub it in that *she* was a witness and *they* were not. "She rousted me out of my nook to explain it all. And she wasn't done until after the wixting-hour, mind you."

Sarvet plucked one of the hoolinberries deliberately from her plate and looked it over slowly, noting its fine crimson-purple color, its sweet floral scent.

Amara followed the fruit with her gaze all the way to Sarvet's lips. "Oh, can't I have one of yours? Please?"

A platter of pickled greens was making its way down the long table. Brionne seized it ostentatiously and flourished it under Amara's nose. "Gundru, Amara?"

"Oh, you!" But she laughed and served a healthy scoop of the slimy mass onto her plate. And then did likewise for her companions. "You know gundru's *so good* for you! I insist!"

Brionne giggled, and Sarvet found her friend's upbeat humor contagious. A chuckle escaped her lips, banishing the last of her tension. Of course, she actually liked gundru. Amara didn't, but she was being charitable about it.

"So!" Amara swallowed a bite of greens, grimaced, and continued, "Guess what Sister Kilti told me last night."

"What?" asked Brionne obligingly.

"There's another, *more* secret ritual within the secret rite!" Amara straightened and widened her eyes. "What do you think of *that*?!"

"After the blessing? Part of the communion?"

"Uh, huh."

"You'll get in trouble, if you tell us about it." Sarvet doubted that would stop Amara. And she *was* curious. What did happen during the communion that the witnesses witnessed? That she and Brionne – and all the other little girls, the "innocents" – would not? And what might this extra secret part be?

"Well, I'm not going to tell you *about* it. Just what it's called: the adoration! And only the Holy Caller attends."

"So all the witnesses file out? Just like the innocents do earlier?" That made Sarvet feel better. Amara would still not know everything. But what *was* the adoration? And the communion? She wished Amara *would* gossip about this.

"Yup. But Sister Kilti did tell me what happens! It sounds . . ." uncharacteristically, Amara trailed into silence. "Well, you'll find out next year."

"Next year!" Brionne burst out. "Amara Iteydet-spring! You have to say more than that!"

"No." Their friend's face grew solemn. "Sister Kilti made me see . . . that I could really ruin things for you, if I shared too much. So I won't."

"Hmh!" Sarvet looked at Brionne. They nodded at one another, and then turned back to Amara. Doubtful they could make the older girl disgorge more, but they could surely make her pay for telling only enough to tease! *Let's see, first I'll rag her about the spot on her face last week. Then I bet Brionne will bring up the time she walked in on Puheliet in the dump-buckets. And I can think of at least four more embarrassing moments. Excellent!*

Amara took it all in good part, but Sarvet refused to stop – or stop egging on Brionne – until Sister Piha directed everyone into the calling-hall for father-coming.

The sun was finally up, its light glowing dimly through the creamy leather window coverings, dispelling the shadows cast by the oil lanterns. Three candelabra on the sacred table held thickets of candles that would be lit at the start of the linking ceremonies. First this more contemplative interval must pass. Sister Piha was calling on Sias to guide their meditations on the active principle. Mother Johtaia gave a homily, reminding her listeners that chastity should not be prudery. The Holy Caller chanted the *Calling Song* and then commended the gathered sisters to silence and reflection. Sarvet closed her eyes obediently.

So what about this much vaunted "active principle"? Surely it was just doing things. And why was it always coupled with brothers? Sarvet was sure the men and boys of Tukeva-lodge were active. They must have to clean and cook and knit and herd-lure just like the women and girls did here. And the brothers ran a sawmill in the valley. But the sisters of Nottkia-lodge ran a tannery. Surely the mother-lodges were every bit as "active" as the father-lodges.

And yet . . . there was something different about the fathers. And the brothers. Not so much the babes who still lived with their mothers at Kaunis-lodge, but the big boys who'd transferred to Tukeva. And the men. It wasn't just that they were taller and broader and had such deep voices. There was an . . . *energy* to them that was . . . powerful . . . compelling . . . exciting? Sarvet shivered. *This is what Brionne was trying to talk about earlier, wasn't it? I wanted to shut her up.* Sarvet still didn't want to think about it. And yet she did.

What was her first experience of fathers? She didn't really need to ask that question. She knew the answer. *I'm just delaying.* She'd been little, really little. *How many years did I have then. Maybe five?* It was one of her earliest memories. She was sitting in a clump of alpine flowers making a chain from the blooms, carefully selecting all the pink ones, when a shadow fell over her. She'd looked up to see . . . a father looming against the sky. He seemed as tall as the clouds, and his bearded face scared her.

"Sarvet?" His voice was gentle and his eyes kind.

He knelt so that she wouldn't have to crane her neck to look at him. "Do you remember me?"

She didn't, but her fear ebbed. He looked nice.

"I'm Ivvar, your mother's linking-brother."

She still didn't remember him, but she held up her flower chain to show him. It was nearly done.

"Beautiful," he told he. "Would you make one for me?"

And she did, a yellow one, not pink.

He'd just draped it around his neck and was thanking Sarvet when her mother arrived, hot and bothered and annoyed. "You shouldn't be here," Paiam declared.

"I've a right." His voice was equable, but he stayed seated on the grass.

Paiam went on to argue with him. Sarvet couldn't recall the words, but Paiam's rage seemed to cover another feeling. *She would have been crying, except that Paiam never cries.*

Sarvet did remember the end of it. While Paiam stood by in fury, Ivvar had taken his daughter kindly in his arms and kissed her forehead. His lips were warm and dry. "Goodbye, little Sarvet. I'll love you forever."

"You're going?" He'd been a fun play fellow. It seemed a shame to lose him just when she'd found him.

"Yes, I'll be living at Rakas, not Tukeva, now. The brothers of Rakas visit a different mother-lodge."

"Oh." She'd been placid then, accepting his farewell. Now . . . now she felt differently. *Paiam drove him away, shun her! I could have been like Amara and Brionne, seeing my own father several times each year, if it hadn't been for her.* With a small shake of her shoulders, Sarvet opened her eyes.

Her mother was seated on the bench in front of her, a little to the right. She had the same expression on her face that Sarvet felt leaving her own features: faint distaste mingled with longing. Sarvet winced. *I don't want to be like her.* She looked away. Brionne, on one side, was staring at the floor and wiggling her foot, bored. Amara, to the left, was rapt, lids closed on some private exultation. Sister Mieha, one of the novitiates, positively glowed. Whatever *she* was contemplating was . . . inspiring. Sarvet looked away, embarrassed, and caught Brionne doing the same. Her friend stifled a giggle. *I'm ready for this to be over.*

Sister Piha brought the meditation to an end with the deep, low hail of the alpenhorn. Sarvet filed out quietly to the porch with all her lodge-sisters. The overcast from the evening before had dissipated, but the day was merely breezy, not gusty. The snowy slope of their mountain, as well as the peaks across the valley, sparkled under the wintery sun.

The brothers of Tukeva-lodge were close, winding up the path below the smokehouse. They were singing, fitting the rhythm of their steps to that of their glad voices. Sarvet craned from side to side, trying to peer around Brionne. Ivvar would not be among them. He never had been in all these years. But . . . was Nial somewhere in that long line of men and boys? *Shun it!* She couldn't *see*. Then Brionne made room for her at the rail, and she had a clear view. There were Gunnar and Eetu, Nial's friends. But where was Nial himself? She bit her lip. Was he still away on his wanderyar? *It's been more than twelve months. He left before last Other-joy. I thought the wanderyar lasted exactly a year.* But he wasn't there. Could something have happened to him? Out in the wide world beyond the Fiordhammars?

Brionne started bouncing on her heels. "I see him! I see him!" she squealed, and then clapped a hand to her mouth. *Nial?* Sarvet grabbed her arm. It really wouldn't do, if Brionne hurtled down the porch steps to greet the brothers on the path. *They're* supposed to approach *us*. But where did Brionne see Nial?

"Sarvet, Vaino is back!"

Oh. Not Nial. Sarvet sagged. She'd really hoped . . . not just to see her brother-friend, but to talk with him about some of the things that confused her so. He didn't have to live with Paiam – she deliberately used her birth-mother's *name* rather than her kinship – the way Sarvet's lodge-sisters did. He wouldn't alternate between pained silences and feeble excuses. But she wasn't to have the benefit of his thinking. He hadn't yet returned to his father-lodge.

She stopped paying attention. The ritual greeting between Mother Johtaia and Father Biejan, the symbolic offering of pannkuja to each brother as he stepped onto the porch, and the formal presentation of the sister-novitiates to the brother-novices all passed her by.

She emerged from her disappointment in the calling-hall. The candelabra had been lit. Waves of heat rolled out from the fires in the twin hearths beyond the sacred table. Sister Valitte had already pronounced the blessing on the prospective linkings. The disrobing was about to begin.

Each brother-novice bowed to his bride, gently took her hands and turned them palm up. She, in turn, slowly unbuttoned his sweater-tunic. The men were hot from their climb and the warmth of the fires. Getting out from under the thick wool must be a relief, thought Sarvet. *Why do they have to stay in it until now?*

The removal of garments was a deliberate act, considerate, almost a courtship. Sarvet glanced at Brionne again. She was fidgeting, eager for the dismissal of the innocents that would come soon. But a rising tension swept over the witnesses who would stay. What would they witness? Sarvet felt a tingling in her core. She wished she could stay. She also wished she were bored like Brionne, like she had been last year at this point. She wished Nial were here, sitting with the other brothers across the aisle on the benches there.

Then the sister-initiates were standing in their thistle-silk shifts, and the brother-novices were down to their smocks and braies. Sister Piha intoned the dismissal, and Sarvet found herself in the gallery amidst a cluster of girls and boys her age and younger. Brionne, assigned several toddlers for watching, gathered her charges and herded them toward the nursery-hall.

Sarvet turned toward the front portal. She felt hot and prickly and irritable. *I'm not a witness, not a child-minder, not a goatherd, not a kitchen maid. Does Sister Aidnu think that just because I'm lame I can't do any chores that require standing?* It was true she couldn't run after a straying youngster or goat, but even Paiam – *Mother* – urged her to exercise each day.

Someone behind her jostled her elbow as she paused before the coat pegs. The next instant she was engulfed in an energetic, comprehensive embrace and swept off her feet. "Sarvet! There you are!" It was Nial. But, goodness, a Nial much taller, much broader, and *bearded*! She was laughing and hugging him back. *He's here! He's here!*

"Sarvet, where can we go to talk? I have so much to tell you!"

They ended up under the pines behind the lodge, the spot she'd imagined occupying alone. *He's here! But why am I so happy?* She didn't know. She didn't care. It just was so.

"Shouldn't you be in the calling-hall?" she probed. "Or do you have to be older to witness, when you're a brother?" He must be – she calculated – nineteen. She would witness three communion celebrations by that age.

"The father-lodges in the south celebrate Other-joy a month earlier," he explained easily. "I've already been through the whole rigamarole this year. Besides . . . banging open the door amidst communion? Father Biejan would never forgive me."

She giggled.

So he'd witnessed. Her eyes fell. What did he think about the secrets Amara had spoken of? He seemed pretty casual and unconstrained about it all. She looked up again. He was surveying her. "You've grown . . . pretty, Sarvet. In these fifteen months since Ionaber year. Taller, too." He smiled. She felt herself flushing. How did he stay so calm? Seem so grown up? Is that what a wanderyar did? *I want one!*

"You've changed too," she ventured. His black curls – wooly like hers – were the same, and his hazel eyes. But the rest! She wouldn't have known him. Except she did. "I . . . feel a little strange," she confessed.

He laughed. "I feel a bit strange myself. I keep tripping over my own feet, when I'm not careful. Ilggai" – his father – "says I grew so fast my limbs forgot how to find each other." He settled back against the most massive tree bole. "Just this morning, emerging from my tent, I managed to catch both front guy-lines and bring the whole thing down."

"Is that why you were late?" She couldn't really believe the mishap. He didn't seem clumsy. In fact, he seemed more at ease in his body than ever before.

"Oh, no. It took me no time at all to get it back up. The true problem was young Oavan."

"Oavan?" She still felt strangely shy, reluctant to pelt him with either questions or tales of her own doings. *He must think I've grown stupid . . . as well as . . . did he really say I was pretty?*

She managed another glance at him. He showed no signs of anything except enjoying her company.

"Oavan's just arrived from his foster-change," Nial explained. "He's little – just thirty months – and he misses his mother."

"And?" She tilted her head.

Nial grinned. "And he's spirited. And spoiled. And when he was presented with travel tack and fried jerky for breakfast – instead of his usual pannkuja and cloudberries – he threw the father of all tantrums. He was still screaming and writhing when it was time to start for Kaunis-lodge, so I volunteered to stay behind with him. He calmed down soon enough once we were the only ones in camp. But I figured I'd better get some food into him before I carried him here, or there'd just be trouble again." He leaned forward to wink at her, clasp her hand, then let it go. "Ilggai vows he should have sent me off on my wanderyar sooner. He complains: 'If I'd known you'd mind the foster-babes, tromp the wool-bales, and mend the roof with enthusiasm instead of groans . . . you'd have gone at thirteen!'" Even she knew that boys didn't set out until they were fifteen, and many waited for sixteen or seventeen.

"So . . . what did you see? In your wanderyar? Where did you travel first?" She wanted simply to hear his voice, but the tale of his adventures proved enthralling. He'd left the Fiordhammars as soon as he got far enough north to skirt the settled lands of the Silmaren vales and head west to lumber territory. The saw mills were very like those of the Hammarfolk, just larger, but the people dwelt in treehouses or cabins up on stilts.

"And they live man and woman together!" he told her. "Linked for all their years, not just the month of a sweet-moon, as we are." That sounded bizarre. How could the women bear to leave their sisters? And the man, his brothers?

"Did you talk with them?"

"I stayed with a family that needed a 'boot-boy,' because their oldest son was laid up with a broken foot."

She felt her eyes widening. "Were they nice?"

"Oh, Sarvet!" The boyish tone was back in his voice. "I wish you could meet them. Them . . . and all the other friendly folk I encountered. It really is a big world out there. Big . . . and wonderful!"

She wished she could too. Why *couldn't* girls have wanderyars? They *should*.

Nial had continued west from the lumber country, all the way over the Tahdenfiall peaks into Trommeland, where the Trummor-folk built towering totem poles painted in garish reds and oranges and blues, and bathed by sitting naked in piping hot steam huts. Finally he'd circled east again, passing through the ruins of a Ghriana delving on his return trip over the mountains.

"There was the strangest pool there." His gaze had gone distant. "It showed me waking dreams of . . . I hardly know what." Would he say? Find words for the strangeness? Somehow she wanted to know.

"There was a Fatherly Caller . . . he looked a lot like me . . . but he had your eyes . . . and he was older. He was searching ancient hieroglyphs in a natural sandstone maze open to the sky." Nial twitched himself free of this vision and relayed more of his journey. "Have you heard of the Reindeer People?"

Sarvet shook her head no.

"They're on a perpetual wanderyar, traveling from grazing glade to grazing glade, always seeking fresh moss for their herds. They beat wide, flat drums – as wide as they are tall – to frighten away the Deathwind

Woman. And they eat fried bone-marrow, blood sausage, and blood pancakes."

She swallowed down an incipient nausea. "Did you . . . ?"

"It was good. Really." He smiled. "But, you know the oddest thing, Sarvet? The really oddest thing was coming home again. I expected to discover astonishing things on my wanderyar. And I did. But home looks pretty astonishing, too."

He paused, studying the sky. It was blue and clear, but its stillness had become breezy, and a line of cumulous was visible beyond the farther peaks.

"I'd thought the Hammarlending tradition was *the* way to live. That other ways were wrong. And some of them might be, but the ones I saw are just as normal as ours.

"In fact" – he sat up abruptly to be sure of her attention – "some of the wrong ways might be right here in our own lodges!" He sounded indignant.

Now, there was a startling idea. But she didn't feel startled. *I'd say my own mother's way is one of those wrong ones.* "What do you mean?" she asked.

"Rakas-lodge was my first stop back in the Fiordhammars. They would have seemed perverse before my wanderyar, but" – he grinned – "after? . . . well, not so much. Their sister-clan is Iloisetlodge, and the two chalets are so close they share the same smokehouse, spring-house, and byre! Pretty unusual for us, but remarkably like the Silmarish, the Trummors, and the Reindeer People. They even have the linking sacrament more than thrice a year at Other-joy and Mother's Bounty and Long-dark."

His mouth tightened. "It was Jakkiat-lodge that bothered me. They don't have a sister-clan. They don't celebrate Other-joy. And they believe women are vessels of evil.

"The brothers seemed . . . inflexible, joyless . . . even mean. Not all, but . . . too many. And they seem wronger than Rakas-clan and Iloiset-clan." He shook his head again. Smiled. "Never mind. The Jakkiat-brothers might have problems, but most folks are splendid! My travels were fabulous! And it's good to be home."

He took her hand again, this time holding onto it. His fingers were warm and strong. "But what about you? You've let me talk on forever. I wanted to tell you . . . well, all that and more, but I didn't mean to hog the whole conversation." He studied her face. His own changed. "What's wrong, Sarvet?"

How did he know? She'd been smiling, enjoying the marvels he related, not thinking about . . . things she didn't want to think about. But she'd wanted to consult him, and here he was, evincing warm concern for her. Perhaps it was time to think about . . . stuff.

She'd tell him. Well, not everything. Her mother's tears in the night before the Evener sheep-luring, Paiam's ceaseless prayers to the Divine Mother, and her wistful longing for the ancient days when sisters were said to birth daughters without linking seemed . . . too perverse, too private to put words to. But there were plenty of more normal grievances. Where to start? Maybe with yesterday's spat?

"I know I'm lame," she began abruptly, "and that there are things I can't do well enough to do at all. Like taking the goats up to the high pastures or hauling hay bales in the byre. But I'm strong, and a lot of the chores . . . well, it might hurt some to see me moving in halting jerks, but I *can* do it."

Nial nodded – thank Sias *without* any pity on his face, just listening – and allowed her to free her hand for gesturing.

"But *Paiam* has decided that just about any task that requires more than sitting is too much for me. So she petitioned Sister Aidnu to excuse me from kitchen duty, milking, and gardening. Without even asking *me* about it." Sarvet could hear the outrage creeping past her determination to talk calmly. "Maturely," as her mother – *Paiam* – would say.

"The byre-sister and the green-sister know me well enough that . . . well, they evaded promising her anything and checked with me. So I'm still taking my turn at milking and weeding and wilding. But when I reported to the kitchens yestermorn, Cook Unni simply dismissed me!"

"Umh . . ." Nial grimaced. "Surely your lodge-mother?"

"She asked me if I liked cooking. And . . . I don't really. So then she explained that if I were longing to chop cabbages and mix pannkuja, she'd overrule my mother, but since I wasn't she preferred to honor Paiam's vulnerability." Sarvet vented a grunt of frustration. "I'm fifteen, for Sias' sake! Nearly sixteen! I'll be old enough to witness in five weeks! And Paiam may be vulnerable, but this is *my* life, not hers!"

"You need a wanderyar." Nial shrugged. "Oh, I know that . . . isn't possible. Girls don't. But that's part of why boys get one. Fathers have a hard time seeing that their sons aren't young ones anymore. And . . ." – he hesitated, then continued – "the boys usually can't see that while they can do *most* things, they aren't yet able to manage *everything*. Of course, by the time they finish their traveling, they *can*!" He grinned, taking the sting out the implication that she wasn't yet fully grown.

"Speaking from experience?" she asked, feeling the corners of her mouth turn up. Maybe things weren't so desperate. At least Nial understood.

"Of course! Ilggai was still trying to tell me when to get up and when to go to sleep last year."

"Oh! Paiam does that too! And when to go to branching-hall for daily postures, and to be thorough about my dawn-sequence while I'm at it. But to make sure Brionne carries the full milk buckets for me and not to go farther than the ice-rock when I'm wilding for nettles. Urgh!"

"It's irksome," Nial agreed. "But, Sarvet, there's something more that's bothering you, isn't there?"

She nodded and felt tears prick her eyes. "Brionne's mother is a lot the same way, just . . . not quite so bad." She swallowed, trying to swallow down the sudden grief in her throat, then burst out: "I understand why Paiam overprotects me, but I wish she wouldn't! Why can't she see all the things I *can* do? All the clever ways I get around the things that might stop me, but don't?"

Nial slid over to her tree trunk and put an arm around her shoulders, wordless.

She turned in the loose circle of his embrace to demand fiercely: "You don't see me as broken, do you?"

She felt the tremor of his stifled laugh – reassuring her again that he didn't pity her. "Of course not! Sarvet, your mother can't possibly see you so! You're a capable young woman who's dealt well and thoroughly with a challenging physical impediment. Paiam should be proud of you!"

Sarvet untwisted herself and leaned against his solid torso, relaxing. "I don't think she is, somehow."

"Really?" Nial looked startled.

"Just yesterday, when she was scolding me for being three skeins short of my spinning quota – I'd spent too much time in the byre and then in the branching-hall – she broke off criticizing and suddenly started apologizing to me for . . . for being too fond of her linking-novice." Sarvet felt herself blushing. She hadn't meant to share this. Too embarrassing! "Paiam believes I suffered my birth injury because she loved my . . . father. That if she'd hated poor Ivvar, I'd be sound and whole." She stared fixedly at the pine needles under her felted boots. Maybe she should have kept safely to talk about Nial's wanderyar. He couldn't help her. And airing this wound . . . oh, Sias! what if Paiam were right?

"Sarvet . . ." He waited until she finally looked up. His eyes were serious, caring, but not patronizing. "You're not broken. Hear me?"

She nodded, felt another sob rising in her throat, and swallowed angrily.

"And your mother loving your father has nothing to do with your lameness. It doesn't work like that."

"I didn't think it did." She sighed. "It's just . . . that Paiam can be so . . . I don't know."

"Yeah. I know. Your mother is . . . I don't know either."

Sarvet gave a shaky laugh. Nial might know a lot, but he still didn't know everything. Thank Sias!

"But, Sarvet, you're the one with the right ideas in this. Hold fast to that! She can't limit you forever. And then . . . it *will* be your life. Make sure you're ready to live it your way, not hers." His lips tightened. "Promise?"

She nodded, feeling an answering determination rising in her.

Then Nial stiffened and muttered . . . something. Had he cursed? Maybe not, because his next words seemed less agitated than those following an oath should be. "Good. You can do it, you know."

She nodded again.

"Good," he repeated. "Because Paiam just rounded the corner of the lodge, and she's headed our way. She looks . . . steamed," he added.

"Has she seen us?" Maybe Paiam was merely fetching an extra measure of water from the spring house. The break in the weather – certainly a temporary thing – meant the stream was releasing a trickle of moisture, and spring water tasted nicer than melted snow.

"Yes."

"Shun it!" Sarvet often preferred to avoid her mother these days, but this had to be the ultimate in moments she didn't want Paiam intruding on. "Let's hide!"

"Um. I don't think that'll work." She could feel Nial chuckling. His ability to see the humor of her involuntary suggestion bolstered her courage. She turned her head.

Her mother hadn't stopped even to put a coat on. Of course, it was warm for Falnary, and the sisters' sweater-tunics and shoulder-hoods kept the cold out, but the anger prompting Paiam's haste was clear in the stomp of her feet and the jerk of her elbows. Her energy brought her up with her daughter in a very few moments.

"Good nooning, Nial Ilggai-spring," Paiam ground out. The words were courteous, but her tone was not. "I need a few words with Sarvet." Her curt gesture invited Nial to leave.

He returned the greeting, but ignored her invitation. "I'd say you need solace and a smidgeon of serenity before you attempt those words," he observed.

The advice did not go down well. Paiam's nostrils grew pinched and white with the force of her inhalation. "I know very well what I need, and it isn't your opinion or your presence, Tukeva-lodger. Now, go!"

He did stand, drawing Sarvet up with him. Paiam had stopped a little downhill from them, so this put their heads above hers. Nial addressed Sarvet: "What would you prefer? Will my staying help or not?"

His refusal to acknowledge Paiam's authority, along with the sight of his hand holding Sarvet's, seemed to enrage a woman already enraged to her utmost. She abruptly transferred her attention to her real target.

"What are you doing here like this? Neglecting your chores and canoodling like an novitiate. How dare you! Get back to the lodge this instant, young sister, and into the spinning room where you belong."

Except Sarvet didn't belong there. The noontide dinner came next, and no one was doing any but rock-sure necessities on Other-joy. Certainly not spinning. She put her chin up, finding – maturity? – in the firm clasp of Nial's fingers. "Nial is our guest," she reminded her mother, "and my friend. I'd planned to attend him in the refecting-hall." With her steady gaze she dared Paiam to continue scolding.

But Paiam needed no dare. "Guest or no, *you* will be attending no one! You'll catch up on the skeins you left undone yesterday, Sarvet *Ivvar-spring*, if I have to get Mother Johtaia herself to rule so!"

The fight devolved from there, with Nial on the sidelines, opening and closing his hands in uncertainty about what to do. This conflict was beyond him! Paiam went so far as to seize her daughter's arm, and Sarvet lost her Nial-gifted cool. She was screaming a threat to petition for a fosterer and jerking at her mother's clutching grasp, while Paiam jerked back and promised a curfew lasting until Nerich. Mother Johtaia's voice, unusually stern, interrupted them. "Sisters! Paiam! Sarvet! Stop!"

They did stop. Sarvet felt like someone had doused her with cold rain. Welcome rain. Her throat was hot and scraped. She curtsied to her lodge-mother, noticing that Paiam managed the obeisance just as awkwardly as her daughter.

Mother Johtaia nodded to Nial. "I'll sort this, Brother. Perhaps you'd care to join your lodge-mates for dinner." She smiled. "Not to worry. I'll send Sarvet out to your table presently."

Apparently that was sufficiently reassuring, because Nial ceased shifting from foot to foot as though he might sling Sarvet over his shoulder and physically carry her away from her maternal attacker. "You alright?" he asked her.

She was shaking, but she trusted Mother Johtaia. "This might take a while," she answered obliquely. Would he catch her unasked worry?

"I'll be there. And sip sweetleaf tea while you dine, if it takes a *long* while."

A sigh puffed out of her. She nodded and watched him lope effortlessly – so effortlessly – down the slope toward the lodge. The clouds were thickening above the distant peaks visible beyond the nearer ridge. The air smelled like snow.

Mother Johtaia surveyed Paiam for a long moment. Sarvet's mother was scrubbing her hair back from her face. The long, wooly ropes were youthfully dark, but her reddened eyes were . . . old? Sarvet squelched the nascent pity rising in her. *I can't start making allowances for her the way everybody else does, or she'll swallow me whole.* She gritted her teeth.

"Come, Sisters." Mother Johtaia's voice turned matter-of-fact. "The sooner we settle this, the better."

"I'll deal with my daughter myself, thank you." Paiam straightened her shoulders, pulled the cowl of her hood back up, and conspicuously dug her heels into the pine needles.

Johtaia's left eyebrow flew up, but her expression remained warm. "You may tell me so in my counsel-haven." And her authority held, because Paiam did follow.

Sarvet eluded her mother's reaching hand. The snow beyond the shelter of the pines wasn't deep, and she didn't need help. Paiam shrugged and desisted. They accomplished the short walk to the back porch in silence.

Johtaia's counsel-haven was a cozy room near the back door. All its chairs featured armrests and patterned, red wool cushions, with knitted afghans tossed over their backs. The fire in its small hearth had been newly fed, and Sister Kemra placed a tray with a steaming teapot and three mugs on the table before she left them.

Mother Johtaia poured out and got straight to the point. "This isn't the first time, Paiam." She tilted her head. "Care to tell me about it?"

"No." Sarvet's mother flushed. Her tone was curt.

"Very well. I'll ask your daughter."

Paiam drew in a sharp breath. "I *am* her birth-mother."

"Yes, and I am her lodge-mother. I owe a duty to each of you." Johtaia smiled. "Come, Paiam, let me in on this."

Paiam's list of her daughter's offenses was accurate in so far as the facts went. Sarvet did speed through her spinning. She hated the hand loom, a new implement to be learned. She lost herself in the legends recorded on the scrolls Sister Piha lent her. And she spent more time out of doors than Paiam considered proper. But the interpretation that went with them: disobedience, rebellion, lack of cooperation, and insistence on having her own way?! *She wants to control me completely. Any time I stray from her strict orders, I'm defiant.* Sarvet clamped down on her impulse to argue. Mother Johtaia's swift, sidelong glance meant Paiam might not have this all her way.

"I think you love your daughter very much."

Huh? How in the north did Mother Johtaia translate "she's contrary and unruly" into "you love your daughter very much"?

But Paiam gulped, nodded, and abruptly buried her face in her hands.

Huh. So "contrary, unruly" did apparently mean "love her." But it wasn't reasonable. *Her love is strangling me!*

Johtaia was still focused on her mother. Her voice grew gentler still. "What is it that worries you so?"

Paiam's face emerged from her palms, tear-streaked. Her reply was a whisper: "That she'll get hurt."

Johtaia folded her upper lip over her lower, stifled a sigh. "It hurts when someone we love gets hurt, yes."

"I'm not going to let it happen!" Paiam's voice was low, but fierce.

Johtaia nodded. "Let's hear what Sarvet has to say. Can you listen, Paiam?"

Sarvet watched her mother's openness retreat at this reminder that her daughter *was* present. "I think I know what she'll say, but perhaps you don't."

"Let's pretend that neither one of us knows. Because . . . perhaps . . . we don't. Will you try, Paiam?"

Sarvet's mother nodded.

"Good." Johtaia turned to Sarvet. "What happened after the blessing? When you left the calling-hall?"

Sarvet wriggled her shoulders. Surely talking about Nial was the wrong thing to do. But . . . if Mother Johtaia thought she should risk it . . . well, she would.

"I was disappointed, because I was expecting Nial to be back from his wanderyar, and I thought he wasn't."

Paiam's face looked wooden, but Sarvet turned her eyes back to Mother Johtaia and went on. "I was angry about . . . yestermorn" – the lodge-mother nodded, so she understood the reference – "and I wanted to be alone to think about it. But then Nial came after all! And I thought it might help to talk to him about it." She stared at her tea, not wanting to see Paiam's condemnation. "And it did help! Or, at least, it did until . . ." she trailed off. Mother Johtaia must have had a clear view of their conflict while she traversed the slope from the lodge to the pines.

"How long have you known Nial, Sarvet?"

Now she's using her gentle tone on me! But maybe some of it would rub off on Paiam. "We were really little when we met. He'd gotten separated from his minder and was scared. So Sister Lempea, who was minding me, just added him to the group. He taught us how to play leap-squirrel." She smiled at the memory.

"So he's an old and good friend."

"Yes. He is." She'd never put it quite that way to herself, somehow. She saw him only thrice each year – at Other-joy, Long-light, and Giving-day – but she shared her thoughts with him more than with . . . anyone. *Brionne and I do things together. And we both enjoy Amara's liveliness, her jokes, her singing. But I'm closer to Nial. Huh.*

Mother Johtaia addressed Paiam again. "Nial is a kind and reliable young man, but I think this friendship bothers you a lot."

Paiam's hands jerked. "Sisters shouldn't *be* friends with brothers," she grated.

Mother Johtaia looked surprised. *How could she not know?* Sarvet pushed the afghan she'd pulled over her knees off her lap. The hot tea had warmed her up. *I guess Mother has kept her – fear? – of men secret.*

"Why not, Paiam?"

"*Sarvet* shouldn't be," Paiam corrected herself.

The lodge-mother merely tilted her head.

"Only loss and pain and sorrow will come of it. *I* know! And I *am* her mother, Johtaia." So, Paiam wasn't saying her real objection. Sarvet sighed softly. *Why did I hope she might? It wouldn't change anything.* Except . . . maybe it would have, if her mother would take someone other than her daughter into her confidence.

"I won't force you to share your heart's keys, Paiam, but Sarvet is in her wixting years. The guiding of her is now shared between you and me and other sisters with authority." Johtaia met Paiam's eyes straightly. Would Paiam acknowledge her prerogative? Yes, she dipped her gaze.

"And I think Sarvet will benefit from my support. That *is* my charge."

"What is your ruling?" Paiam remained angry, but not defiant.

Mother Johtaia smiled. *Amazing how she could be sympathetic to both contestants when sisters were at odds. Or even when she disagreed with one. Or both!* "I will have more than a single ruling, but this is the first." She returned her attention to Sarvet. "Brothers and sisters do well to be friends. I think you already know this, and that is well. But now I pronounce Nial to be other-brother to you as well. You may trust in your trust for him."

Oh! Sarvet had never dreamed so far ahead as to imagine who her linking-brother might be. In fact, she'd imagined she'd never have one – just as she'd told Brionne. But now Nial would be one of the choices offered her . . . when the time came. It felt strange. Very strange, but right. Her heart lightened inside her.

Paiam's nostrils were white again, but she said nothing. Mother Johtaia was well within her warrant.

"This pleases you?" Johtaia's gaze on Sarvet was loving.

Sarvet managed a nod. She was too happy, too surprised, for words.

"Good. But before I make my second ruling, I have another question for you." She interrupted herself to pour more tea for everyone. "Sarvet, it can be scary to dream big dreams. There are real dangers. What if you let yourself know a wish that you can't live without, once you know it?

"But the rewards of dreaming big are often worth the risk. Without dreams, we settle for far less than we need to." Johtaia paused, checking to be sure Sarvet understood her. (Or to give Paiam a chance to prepare for what came next?) Sarvet nodded, quelling an unlikely hope. *Can she mean –? Is it possible –?*

"So, Sarvet, I'd like you to do some big dreaming. What if you could change anything? What if you could do anything? What if you had all the support you needed to try something amazing?

"Think on those ideas.

"And then dare to dream. How might your life be different? What new experiences might this year bring? What is your deepest desire?"

Sarvet studied the lodge-mother's face. Johtaia was in earnest. This was real. Sarvet could ask something bold, something outside of convention, something unheard of – and be heard. *Did* she dare?

"Tell me," invited the lodge-mother.

"I want a wanderyar," Sarvet announced sturdily. "Just like the brothers. Where I travel from lodge to lodge – mother-lodge to mother-lodge – or even farther, if that seems right."

"No!" Paiam jerked to her feet, spilling tea from the mug clutched in her right hand. "This is absurd!" She rounded on Mother Johtaia. "Now, see what comes of encouraging her! I told you!"

The lodge-mother was nonplussed.

She swallowed, then spoke. "I'll admit I'd envisioned something a little more within bounds. A visit to Siajotti-lodge" – where the sisters maintained and added to a repository of scrolls recording Hammarleeding traditions and legends – "or the request for a fosterer. Or even" – Johtaia pinned Paiam with a stern stare – "an interval of ritual restraint to allow her mother to cool. But this . . ."

Sarvet's neck bent. So, her answer had been too daring. The lodge-mother had wanted something bold, but conventional and with precedent, for all her fine words. Perhaps Johtaia had thought she'd meant them, but . . . Sarvet felt thoroughly let down. And yet . . . *shun it! I won't give up!* That little moment of belief – *maybe I can have this* – was infectious. She lifted her head.

"You said to dream big. And I have. I want a wanderyar. Will you not support me?"

Johtaia looked like she'd been punched in the stomach, but before she could find words for dialog, Paiam jumped into her silence. "That's enough, young sister! Even were you a brother, your lameness must keep you home. Request a fosterer if you want, shun it! Demand a restraint, if you must. I don't care at this point. But here you will stay, and that's that!"

Mother Johtaia recovered herself. "Paiam, wait. That was a surprise, yes. And I agree with you that it isn't practical, but let's talk this through. It's not fair to encourage Sarvet to name her desire and then summarily refuse to grant it.

"Sarvet, let's explore what's behind and beneath this wish of yours. Surely there is a less extreme solution that will satisfy your heart."

I don't think so. But what would Johtaia do now? She was in a predicament as much as Sarvet was. Having exposed a wixting-sister to the irrational wrath of her mother, how would she make good on her duty to both? Or would she?

Paiam reseated herself rigidly and mopped at the spilled tea with a tea towel.

Mother Johtaia pursued her point. "Tell me more about what a wanderyar would do for you."

Sarvet lifted her chin. "I'd see new places and new people. I'd encounter folks who wouldn't always be focusing on my weakness and my limits. I'd do for myself, and discover that I *could* do for myself. I'd be a woman, not a girl, when I got back." *And I wouldn't have to fight Paiam every step of the way, because she wouldn't be there.* The most important point of all.

"Hmm, yes, I see."

Maybe she did, but Sarvet doubted it. *I've never doubted the lodge-mother before.* She felt dizzy.

"But, Sarvet, surely a visit to Siajotti-lodge would do all that."

In a small way, yes. But Sarvet wanted the big way. Especially now that she'd tasted the idea. "I've been to Siajotti. Their scrolls . . . opened vast horizons in my mind. But I want horizons that challenge . . . my body!"

"Oh, Sarvet . . ."

Now Sarvet was mad. "Don't you see?! You're doing it too! Deciding for yourself where I am able and where I am not! I want to *fail* sometimes, shun you!"

The lodge-mother was beyond nonplussed this time; she was stunned.

Paiam, sensing that Johtaia had swung to her side in the dispute, spoke more reasonably for the first time since confronting Sarvet under the pines. "When Nial had his wanderyar, he wasn't risking serious injury or worse. You would be. Elder sisters must safeguard younger ones, as well as supporting their drive toward independence. The answer is no, Sarvet."

"Indeed, Paiam is correct in this." Johtaia reclaimed her authority once more. "But, Paiam, something must be done. You don't want your daughter hurt, but *you* are hurting her. Surely you see this."

"Wixting girls are always difficult. I can bear the burden."

"But let's make it easier on you both. I think a sojourn at Siajotti is in order for the short term, while we ponder the long term. The difficulties between you are . . . complex. We'll not solve them in a week, and certainly not in an hour. But you both need some relief now. And a meal!" Johtaia managed a twinkle.

"Sarvet, go get some dinner, child. And then do your packing. I'll send you off tomorrow morning with Sister Kasikira. Paiam, bide a moment with me here, if you will. I'll ask Kemra to bring us food."

Sarvet fled to the branching-hall. No one would think to look for her there. Or hear her, the way they might if she sought refuge in her bednook. The dim, raftered space was cold and empty. She pulled a bolster and two meditation quilts from a cupboard, then curled herself in a nest under a window. One corner of its hide covering had worked loose. Placing her chin on the sill, she could see out. The conifers in the grove behind the hall, long-trunked and thickly planted, showed little snow on the needle carpet between them. The overcast had returned while she debated with her lodge-mother and her birth-mother; the cheery light of direct sun absent, segued into chilly aloofness. She felt blank, hollow.

Johtaia hadn't devised a solution, and there was additional loss in that. *I'd always thought her infallible. Even today, when Paiam attacked me, I was so sure our lodge-mother would sort things out. Even when* she made them worse, there in her counsel-haven, I thought she'd retrieve it all. *But she hadn't.* The proposed journey to Siajotti was no use. The scroll-sisters had been thoroughly indoctrinated by Paiam on earlier visits in how to over-protect Sarvet. All that would happen was that when Sarvet returned, Johtaia would appoint a fosterer. *And I don't want that.* Yes, it would get Paiam off her back. Yes, it would assure her some freedom from Paiam's suffocating concern. But it would also make her birth-mother not her mother. *Her bossing me is the only connection we have left.*

I don't want freedom forced out of Paiam. I want her to grant it. I want her to change. And no one can give me that, except Paiam herself. Except, she can't either. She doesn't know how.

Pain stabbed through Sarvet's numbness. *Why does she have to be so impossible?* So unyielding? So . . . afraid? Hot tears sprang onto Sarvet's cold cheeks, and hot sobs crowded her throat. *Her fear makes me afraid, and if I get any smaller I'll disappear.*

She cried for a while.

The wind picked up outside, swirling a few flakes dropped by the clouds. Sarvet's raw emotion moderated, gave way to thinking. *I know why she's afraid.* She told me last year, at the same time she explained first blood. She said: Don't have a child, Sarvet. Your heart will break, when she suffers.

But she's wrong! She's wrong! It's not my limp that broke her heart. It's her refusal to accept that what I *have* is so much greater than what I *lost*. And her refusal takes even more away.

Sarvet mused on the failed healing-call that came soon after that talk with her mother. Sister Piha had chanted the entire day-long supplication, while Sister Evaia massaged the diseased joints with blessed and sacred anointing oil. Brionne had insisted on attending and prayed from dawn to dusk. *That's what she was crying about this morning.* Sarvet was suddenly sure. *She was crying, because I am still lame.* Awe pervaded her. To have such loyalty in a friend and not quite realize it. Oh, Brionne!

But the supplication, the intense massage, the prayers, and the attempt to forcibly realign her hip and ankle had been worse than useless. Something had given way within the palsied flesh, and she had been months regaining the ability to walk. Even now, her limp was worse than it had been last year.

But she wasn't going to feel sorry for herself. The lesson wasn't that trying always fails. The lesson was: don't chase after past losses. *Try something new.*

And that is what I wanted to do: take what I *do* have and use it to try something new; many things new! Go meet all the strange people and customs and differences in the big and wondrous place our north-lands are. The north-lands that Nial described so vividly. And I still want that. Only I can't have it.

She felt more resigned than desperate.

I suppose I should go scrounge something from the kitchens. Dinner must be long done. She straightened within her cocoon of quilts.

"Oh, Sias! What must Nial be thinking! I never came to him as Mother Johtaia promised."

She jumped to her feet, wincing as the sudden jolt to her stiffened hip and foot brought pain. Ow! She bundled the quilts onto their shelf in the cupboard, shoved the bolster onto its, then lurched onto the porch. On the slope beyond the lodge, brothers and sisters were tossing snowballs at one another, but the rising ground between the lodge and the branching-hall held only one hurrying figure: Nial.

She waited for him.

"Sarvet!" He came leaping up the steps and gripped her shoulders. "What happened? I finally went to your lodge-mother. But why didn't you come eat?" He folded her close, then stepped back to scrutinize her. "You've been crying." He touched a gentle finger to her cheek. "Did the lodge-mother fail your trust?"

"No. Or, rather, yes. But . . . Nial, will you help me?" *Would* he help her? Her thoughts flitted to other times he'd supported her. Every Ionaber during Death-joy, he went aside with her to the Zele-chapel to kneel in meditation, telling over his prayer beads in time with hers, joining his voice to hers in the chant: *we arrive on the waters of birth; we depart across the river of death.* His own choice would surely have been the clapping game preferred by most. Few were the years when he and she were not the sole occupants of Zele's sacred space. (Paiam defied custom and sequestered herself alone at the shrine she kept in her room.)

The laughter of the jumping, spinning celebrants in the adjacent calling-hall was loud, along with their chorused claps and the thump of their feet. The words of their song were eerie – *when will I die?* (clap) *when I am young?* (clap) *at life's end?* (clap) *when I am old?* (clap) *when I am ancient?* (clap) *when tomorrow comes?* (clap) – but their tone, merry. The rattle of their flung pebbles sounded an insistent staccato for living, defying the lassitude of dying. Wouldn't Nial rather be leaping and laughing? She'd almost chosen so last year, but the dry quiet of the chapel drew her. And . . . the daring defiance of death, seizing revelry in its very teeth, scared her. But Nial remained steadfast each year. *Would* he help her now? With this?

Nial looked confused. "Of course, I'll help you. That's what I offered; but what do you need help *with*?"

She drew in her breath. "I'm going on a wanderyar, and I want you to get me a tent and a pack and a bedroll."

Nial's hands dropped to his sides. Then he gripped her shoulders again, giving her a little shake. "You can't! Mother Johtaia never gave you permission for that?"

"No." Her voice sounded forlorn in her ears. *None of that. I'm not waiting on anyone's permission any more.* She lifted her chin and straightened. Her voice came out stronger. "But I'm giving *myself* permission."

Nial was starting to smile. "How can you do that?"

Her lips curved to match his. "But, Nial, anyone can do that any time. I'm *going*."

"Okay." He tipped his head to one side. "And not planning to seek my permission either, huh?"

"Of course not."

He let his hands fall again, but only to abandon his skeptical demeanor. "I think you'll need trail food and coin as well."

"Oh." Her shoulders fell. She could probably find hard tack and jerky in the pantry, but how would she abscond with it through the busy kitchens? And the lowlander Silmarish did use coin, she remembered, but the Hammarleedings did not. Traveling from mother-lodge to mother-lodge would not work, since she went without her lodge-mother's permission. *I need coins, if I leave the Fiordhammars.*

"Sarvet, don't worry. I've got both."

"Oh!"

"And I will help you . . . but . . . can you tell me a little more? More than just you're going? A wanderyar . . . takes preparing, too. Not just going."

"Like linking." Suddenly she felt less embarrassed about linking and communion and adoration – whatever those last two involved. Was it because Nial was now her other-brother?

"Like linking," he confirmed.

"And I don't have any." Somehow she knew he wasn't objecting. This wasn't a prelude to an effort to stop her. *No, he's gong to prepare me . . . as best he can.*

"No, you don't." He hesitated. *Was* he going to stop her? Surely not. Or was his belief in her strength only strong if she didn't test it? He continued: "But with the right supplies – my supplies – you'll be fine. The Silmarish and the Sammiad and the Trummor-folk like wanderers. They'll help you along. And you'll find how to pay your way." His grin dawned. "Come on!"

Would it really be this easy?

Not quite. But it wasn't Nial who would stand in her way. He led her to the path around the grazing bluff – thus avoiding the slope immediately below Kaunis-lodge where the brothers and sisters threw snowballs – and along to the empty brother-camp.

"You'll need my lightest gear," he remarked. "Luckily, I had a notion of trekking to the Tunkahorn on my way home."

"Do you mind –"

"Not a bit." He stopped rummaging in his tent and turned back to face her. Looking up from his knees, he grew suddenly serious. "This is your moment, Sarvet. Like a bird on the wing, you're meant to soar. And I'm going to give you the wrist toss you need for it. It's about time someone did."

"I'm not –"

"Only a fool would think you broken or a burden or dependent." He was fierce. "Never apologize, Sarvet! You're strong and creative and able. Always remember that."

She felt shaken by his vehemence, but a wild exultation rose in her. Her words emerged calm, despite it. "I love you, Nial Ilggai-spring."

He took both her hands in his, turned them over, brushed a light kiss in each palm. "And I love you."

"Is it allowed?"

"Didn't Mother Johtaia just make me your other-brother?"

A short laugh blew out of her. "How did you know?"

"Father Biejan made you my other-sister and . . . I hoped." His eyes were deep and tinged with awe.

"I'm not old enough."

"No. Not yet." He drew her head down, and his lips touched her forehead.

"And I'm still taking my wanderyar!"

A chuckle shook him. "You wouldn't be Sarvet else."

Her scowl became a grin.

Once she was equipped, Nial surveyed her. Following his cue, she inventoried herself: rucksack, bivy, and sleep-sack all of thistle-silk – the latter quilted; oiled ground cloth, water canteen, mess kit, tinder wheel and tinder store; jerky, hard tack, and powdered kerin-herb; snow-shoes, poles, ice-hammer. "I need my coat and gaiters and over-mittens."

"I can get them."

And he did. Plus a small pouch of dried cloudberries and alp pinyons. Her stomach was grateful, since she'd missed the noon meal.

"You must go down, not up, Sarvet. Peak ascensions require a group effort."

"You were headed to the Tunkahorn," she reminded him.

"The valley trail, not the highlands."

"Mmm. Well, I want the lowlands anyway. I want to meet all those interesting people you talked of."

"You will!" His eyes lit. "You will. And Sarvet . . . Sias keep you."

"And you." The formal parting seemed right somehow: not a denial of the new connection she felt for him, but an affirmation – and an acknowledgment of postponement.

She looked back when she reached the valley-rock.

He stood silhouetted against the sky, distant already, but watching for the last sight of her. She waved, waited for his answering salute, and stepped around the curving descent.

I'm away!

And she was. It would be dusk before she could turn onto the Ulko-polku, the trail leading away from Hammarleeding ground toward the Silmarish lowlanders. *But I'm not making camp until then.* The gentler slopes should afford a better spot for pitching her bivy and . . . she craved newness.

When the mountain slopes darkened, and only the clear sky reflecting on the snow allowed her to see, her desire for newness muted to mere stubbornness rather than eager anticipation. A grinding ache pulsed in her right hip, and she narrowly missed tangling her right snowshoe in the left on too many of her limping right steps. Going down was always more painful than climbing. A small level cranny between two half-buried boulders tempted her. Then she spotted the turn-off for the Ulko-polku. *I'll stop as soon as I come to the treeline.* The pine grove sheltering the Kaunis-lodge was an anomaly. All the slopes below it were turf-covered until this lower elevation. *Nial said not to camp directly under any tree branches, but a clearing amongst the pines would be pleasant and safe.*

But it was the trees that were her undoing. With their protection came shadows. She never saw the thin, whippy branch lying across a steep stretch of the trail. An invisible hand seemed to grab her left ankle, wrench her snowshoe sideways, and pitch her downhill with stunning force.

She awoke to burning numbness in her left cheek where it pressed the snow, a bone-deep throbbing in her right hip, and a scary wrongness in her right ankle. Her stomach sickened under the pain, and she hovered on the edge of the black pit from which she'd emerged. *I could die here.* She didn't feel cold – except for the one cheek. Whether it was because of her layered clothing or because pain drove out chill, she didn't know. *I have to move.* But she couldn't somehow. She could feel all her limbs, guessed that with enough will exerted, they would move, but the pain sapped her strength. *I will move. I will move!*

And still she lay unmoving.

A feathery coldness dusted her right cheek. The snowfall she'd smelled earlier had arrived. Her body felt heavy and cooler. She lifted her head a fraction and was surprised by her relief from the icy grating of the half-melted snow against her frozen skin. Her arms were trapped under her torso, and she wriggled them free, then pushed upward. The movement jolted her hip and leg, shooting pain through the entire limb. Her hands slipped, and she found her face planted once more in snow as she grabbed for the source of agony.

When she tried again, she pushed up only enough to free her face and creep herself forward a hand span. *If I could just get to a flatter bit of ground.* The steepness of the trail thwarted her care. Even the minute downhill momentum from inching forward was sufficient to carry her onward in a slippery rush. The bumpy ride provoked a fresh staccato of pain, whiting out all thought.

Coherence returned slowly. *Downhill isn't working. I can't control my descent.* Was there some way to go up instead? She checked her surroundings. Her slide down the trail had brought her to a wider place in the way. Could she reverse herself? Painstakingly she worked herself sideways, learning with each stabbing error how to use her arms and left leg without jolting her right leg. Several times she gave up, but the instinct for survival eventually prevailed after each defeat. Having her head uphill made breathing easier; having her feet downhill increased the intensity of the shrill torment in her ankle.

She lay gasping. Her snowshoes had detached in her fall, her poles, escaped from her grasp; but she wouldn't be standing in any case. *I'll get there crawling,* she told herself, waiting for readiness. It didn't come, but she began her ascent without it: dig in the good foot, push with the good leg, pull with the supporting arms, gasp at the stab of pain brought by movement. One push-pull after another. She didn't stop when she reached the turn-off for home. *If I stop, I might never start again.* Her face was slick with sweat – the result of exertion and pain combined – and her clothes felt warm and soggy. Push-pull, up, flinch. Push-pull, up, flinch.

The snowfall had stopped by the time she reached the fork in the trail below the valley-rock. She halted. *Why am I resting? This is it! I've made it. Turn right. I'm almost home.* Paiam's tense face and voice swam in her memory: Don't have a child, Sarvet. Your heart will break. Your heart will break. Your heart will break.

She wrenched herself violently to the left, stifling her scream at the hot agony this produced. Push-pull, up, *aagh!* Push-pull, up, *ungh! I won't go back! I won't!* Anywhere were better than home.

She lost all sense of time, of place, of self. She was a swirl of hurting, of disorientation, of fury, of stubborn striving ever upward. Another flurry of snowfall came and went. The overcast cleared, but she barely noticed. The stars of the wixting hours pulsed in all their grandeur and glory, heralding promise and hope. Sarvet struggled onward, oblivious.

When she found herself lying on flat turf, an eon later, she faltered. What if flat gave way to down? *I won't go down. I won't go back.* And where had the snow gone? Inching forward on short, resilient grasses and mosses was so much easier than tackling the slippery incline of snow and ice. Where *was* she? She lifted her face.

The moon had set, but starshine illumined the alpine meadow stretching away from her. Black, spangled sky swung dizzily around her, fringed at its lower hem by white ridges in the distance, across great valleys. She'd never climbed so high before. Had anyone in Kaunis-lodge? But where did she go now? There seemed no up accessible, save for an eagle.

As she paused, panting and unwilling to admit defeat, a kind womanly voice sounded in . . . not her ears, but her mind. "Thee must be braver still, brave climber."

What?

Sarvet jerked her gaze to the right. *Had* the silent behest come from her right?

Ah! *There* was up: at the meadow's rim a sheer precipice, black in the night, rose to yet unseen heights, perhaps the peak of this mighty uplift of earth. Could she find a trail, however steep, by which to continue her journey? She renewed her struggle to move. The pain seemed sharper after the brief hiatus, and she was . . . more weary. *I will move.*

But she didn't.

Instead she gazed at the night sky. There was Livli the Skier on the horizon, and the Great Chalice. If it were spring, the sun would be rising. Being winter, the stars reigned supreme, still promising . . . *more than I will ever receive.* She didn't feel defeated, just . . . accepting? *Maybe I've already received . . . enough? Hunh?*

A flutter of movement over the reach of the wide valleys drew her attention. What was it? Eagles and peregrines hunted at dawn and dusk, when the rock doves were active. Sarvet narrowed her eyes. Something winged. Some *three* things winged, yes, but white and gauzy. She pushed upward on her arms to see better, gasping at a stab of extra pain. Not birds . . . no. And big, far bigger than she had first suspected. Were they –? Could they be –? Her lips parted. *Oh!*

The pegasi! The fierce winged horses who defended the sacred precincts of Duoja's immortal spring and who attacked Lagon's demons in the ancient War of the Lodestones. She'd thought them creatures of legend only, but here they soared, strangely transparent and indefinite at their edges – yet real, for all that – riding the air toward her. She stared transfixed.

Nearer and nearer they flew, magnificent wings outstretched, hooves trammeling the breeze in preparation for landing. Then they were down, furling their vast eery wings, galloping across the greensward toward her. Their churning transparent legs shook the ground, their half-seen nostrils flared with aggression, and their pace brought them upon her in an instant. *Will I be trampled?* The lead pegasus gave a ringing neigh and reared to a stop, his muscled forelegs thumping into the grasses beside Sarvet's tense hands.

"You intrude, bold dreamer." The stallion's voice – unheard by the ears, like the mare's earlier – was deep and challenging. "If you've defiance, proclaim it; if a gift, offer it; if a boon sought, beg it. But you may not merely wait on fate here."

Sarvet was shaking, half in awed wonder, half in shock at the thunderous approach of the three steeds. She swallowed, suddenly aware of her dry mouth and throat. Could she form speech?

"For shame, cloud strider." The mare's voice, still kind, bore reproof. "This be no hero, nor foe, nor pretender. She's a true pilgrim, though she knoweth it not, and a small one at that, a mere filly." The pegasus to the right – dancing-friend? – stepped delicately forward. "Canst thee speak, valiant seeker?"

Sarvet found her voice. "No. He's right." She swallowed again. "I do beg a boon."

"Indeed, bright traveler. Yet thee needst no challenge. Be welcome and speak thy prayer."

Sarvet swallowed a third time. Unlike Mother Johtaia, these creatures out of legend would not fail her. Was she ready for the challenges success might bring? Was she ready to ask a second time for the scariest wish of all?

"Grant me health." Her voice wavered. "Grant me vibrant health and steady steps. If you will."

The mare on the left – wind-caller? – eased closer. Her "voice" was lighter – older? – than those of the other two. "Dost thee understand the price of thy request, sweet mountain-child? There is always a cost to any striving."

"I know." Somehow, she did know. And, although she didn't know what cloud strider and dancing-friend and wind-caller would ask of her, she suspected it would be nothing so simple as a barter or trade of help for service or coin. "What must I give?"

Wind-caller's answer stirred her tired hurting limbs like a call to arms. "You must surrender your most cherished defenses, embrace your greatest fears, relinquish the self you are for the one you would become. Will you do this?"

That was comprehensive. Sarvet swallowed yet again before whispering: "I will." And then her arms collapsed, her vision dimmed, and her cheek – turned just in time – pressed damp turf.

Dancing-friend's velvet lips whiffled over Sarvet's jawline. "Hast tried thee too hard, strong seeker! One more effort from thee, and thou shalt rest. Canst thee dare it?"

Sarvet tried to nod, but doubted her head moved at all.

Dancing-friend seemed to intuit her unuttered yes. "Shalt kneel to thee, and then thee must place thine right hand upon my cannon bone."

There was an interval of . . . maneuvering or something. Sarvet scarcely knew. Then a presence and a warmth lay close by her side. She raised her right hand, felt something solid under her palm, and pressed against it.

"Good, valiant trier! Canst thee leap?"

Leap! She'd not have managed that before the failed healing last year!

"The merest intention is enough," dancing-friend assured her.

Sarvet managed to twitch her left foot. And found herself seated on a warm, solid horse back between a blur of wings, unfurling to free dancing-friend's flanks for Sarvet's legs and re-folding to cover them. The dramatic change in position sent an agonizing lancet of pain through Sarvet's hip. She did not fall, but she did slump forward against dancing-friend's mane in a haze of exhaustion.

The pegasus rocked her way to standing in the way of equines. It should have jolted her rider, sending limp Sarvet to grass, but somehow it didn't. Dancing-friend's back and neck felt rock-stabile even as she tipped this way and that. *I am cradled*, thought Sarvet dozily, *like a babe in arms*.

Dimly she sensed the pegasus turning, walking, moving under the stars. The night's sheeny light dimmed – were they passing under a rock arch? – then a warmer glow replaced it.

"Thee must exert thyself once more, brave pilgrim."

"Mmm?" Sarvet felt too sleepy to do anything. Was it the dangerous sleepiness brought on by cold? She almost didn't care. Besides, it was warm here on the pegasus' back inside this grotto.

"Needst not move from mine back, but thy skin must be free of garments."

Even this peculiar request left Sarvet unperturbed. "Mmm."

"Thee climbed a mountain one-legged, little sleeper. Must touch that courage enough to undress now."

Lassitude still claimed her, but Sarvet found her fingers wriggling out of over-mittens and under-gloves, seeking her coat toggles amidst dancing-friend's mane. She let her clothing simply slide down dancing-friend's flanks to the grotto floor. The gaiter and boot on her right foot were hard. *Will I fall?* Somehow she didn't, despite the awkward way she dangled over one side, picking at the laces and attempting to ease the gear off her swollen ankle without jarring it. Renewed pain pierced her hip, but she didn't even slip. *Is there some magic between the wings of a pegasus?* Falling never seemed remotely possible through all the shedding of her layers, including the tricky business of removing her under-trews.

It felt odd to be naked and warm. Even in summer, Kaunis-lodge was filled with cool air, and the switch between nightclothes and day clothes was a chilly proposition. Dancing-friend's hide was smooth as thistle-silk against Sarvet's bare thighs and buttocks. The pegasus was moving again, picking her way down a gentle slope. A generous pool of still water, glimmering in the golden light of the grotto, startled Sarvet awake.

"I can't swim!"

But dancing-friend had already entered the tarn in a gentle surge, and the warm water covered Sarvet's legs, rose to her waist.

"Shalt bear thee up, earth-child. Fear not."

The water was deep, over Sarvet's head if she'd been standing on her own feet, but aback a pegasus she was safe. Dancing-friend waded deeper, and the water reached Sarvet's chest.

"Mayest sleep now, dreaming doer. Thou hast reached haven at last." Dancing-friend's translucent wings lifted up out of the water, apparently (and unexpectedly) dry, screening most of the grotto from Sarvet's view.

But Sarvet was enthralled by the caress of the warm water against her skin, the soothing weight of it on her sore body, the ease of her perch on the pegasus amidst the danger of the pool's depth. She stretched her arms to embrace the ripples when they reached her shoulders, dipped her face to taste them with her tongue: slightly salt, slightly eggy.

"Mmm."

"Is it well, sweet receiver?"

"Yes," she murmured. "Yes." *I've never been this relaxed*, she realized, *ever*. Always, through all her memory, she'd been tense. Resisting pain, resisting being an invalid, resisting favors, resisting . . . *Paiam*. Abruptly she was tense again.

"Let it go," suggested dancing-friend.

But if I let go . . . Paiam will win.

"Oh?"

"I'll never grow up. I'll be her baby forever, her child, her dependent. Spinning and weaving in that close room under her eye, never digging, never hiking, never rolling down the slope. Always working, always trapped!" She felt sobs choking her throat. "I want to be free!"

"Here is freedom." Dancing-friend's words were soft.

"No, it's not! It's danger. Letting go is letting her *in*, and I won't!" Sarvet's tension was growing, and with it came increasing pain. Her right hip and foot were throbbing again, her ankle under assault by sharp wrongness.

Dancing-friend continued moving gently through the water. "What are your dreams for yourself, beloved?"

Oh.

Beyond her wanderyar, she hadn't truly had any. Sarvet's tension ebbed. She thought. What *did* she want for herself? There were decades ahead of her, and wandering for all of them . . . well, she wouldn't see much of Nial.

Nial. Nial was part of her future. She wanted . . . communion with him . . . adoration with him . . . *babies* with him. Terror shot through her, banishing her returning relaxation. My heart will *break*. My *heart* will break. *My heart will break.*

Oh.

She *was* her mother's child.

For all her resistance to Paiam's narrowness, some portion of it had crept within her, nestling in a dark and sacred place, rooting within her soul. She was scared to expand, scared to claim the fullness of bounty available in a life, scared to expect fun, scared to expect pleasure. *I snatch when chance presents an opportunity, but I don't seek any out.* I'm a beggar at the gates of living, just like my mother, and . . . *I do not have to be!*

Her ribs shuddered and hot tears wet her cheeks. She was crying, feeling all her lost moments, feeling the pinch of her own choice of limitation: different from her mother's shrinking, but equally narrow.

She is hot and cramped and tangled, but I am cold and barren and spare. I don't want either; I don't want either. Oh, Mother, Mother.

She was crying more easily now, chest loose in its sobs, throat open.

"We are here," came dancing-friend's whisper.

And they were. Sarvet could feel the cloud strider and wind-caller in her mind along with dancing-friend, wordless yet present, strong and loving and . . . calm. *They trust me,* she realized in surprise. They recognize this battle, and . . . *they have faith I will* win *it,* whatever winning it may be. Her sobs were slowing, stopping. She felt . . . no, not empty. She felt . . . open, clear . . . free! I *am* free. I can . . . make a different choice.

Oh!

I can expand. I can be . . . big! I can grow up. And have a baby. *Babies!* And I can do more. Maybe I'll have more than one wanderyar. Maybe I'll search the oldest scrolls in Siajotti-lodge and discover more legends –

like the pegasi – that are true. Maybe I'll invent a cure for other girls like me who suffer a birth injury. And boys too. Maybe I'll be a hero! Maybe I'll claim my birthright! Maybe . . . I will *live*.

She put her chin up and let the last residual morsels of holding, gripping, and *resisting* go. With it went the armor holding her utter weariness at bay. Sarvet slumped.

"Well done, brave warrior! Well done!" The pegasi's praise carried the force of a shout, in spite of their gentleness.

She found herself smiling, snuggling her cheek in dancing-friend's silken mane.

"Be at peace, pegasus-friend. Be peaceful."

She slept then, vaguely aware of being shifted after an interval from dancing-friend's back to that of wind-caller, and later still to the cloud strider's. They carried her outside and packed her leg and hip and foot in snow at the edge of their grassy meadow, then returned her to the grotto for more watery warmth. She roused only partially for the different measures of the circuit, just enough to make the effort of will that seemed to replace efforts of limb. Hot to warm to cold to hot; friend to caller to strider to friend; inside to outside to inside.

She awoke properly on wind-caller's back in the grotto. Dancing-friend was nudging Sarvet's shoulder with her nose. "Must drink and sup, victorious one."

Sarvet sat up and looked around her. Wind-caller was bedded on a drift of golden moss. Other mats of the fuzzy stuff dotted the grotto floor, and they all glowed. *So that's where the light came from.* She spotted her pack buried under the pile of her doffed clothes and started to dismount.

Dancing-friend stopped her. "Not yet, dreaming healer! Thy foot wilt be ready in time, but must rest a while." Once assured that Sarvet would stay put, the pegasus picked her way around the grotto's pool, gripped a pack strap between her teeth, and hoisted the pack from the piled clothing.

Draining her canteen, Sarvet discovered the unexpected extent of her thirst and wished for more. How could she get a refill, if she were not allowed to walk? And from where? The hot water that soothed her hurts held little appeal for drinking.

"Sup first," instructed wind-caller.

Just as water recalled her thirst, so jerky and hardtack recalled hunger. The dense, resistant texture of the food made for a lot of chewing when she wanted to gobble. Perhaps it was as well that she was forced to go slow.

Refilling her canteen proved involved, but not insupportable. Wind-caller stood with the same rocking motions used by her companions, then carried Sarvet through a curving tunnel that connected the grotto to the outside. It was a gusty day, the wind chasing mare's tail clouds across the endless sky, yielding a rapid flicker of shadow and sun across the meadow. The flanking mountains peaked far below this high sanctuary, and the flower-studded lawn felt like the uttermost top of the world. The magical warm stillness between the pegasus wings held both breeze and chill at bay. Sarvet felt winter's sting only when she stretched out her arm to the snowbank at the meadow's edge, scooping the icy crystals into the wide mouth of her vessel. Dipping the filled canteen in the warm water of the grotto's pool melted the snow just enough to create a refreshing, slushy drink.

Then the healing circuit devised by the pegasi resumed: warm water bath while riding followed by snowpack out of doors. After a third visit to the pool, wind-caller added a new therapy. Sarvet was permitted to recline on a bed of moss while the pegasus healers brushed her injured leg with their wings. It was bewildering to *see* the insubstantiality of their pinions, yet *feel* the real brush of silken feathers against her skin; although little less confusing than the clash of the senses produced by riding their firm backs while seeing the gauziness of their bodies.

A pleasant tickling within Sarvet's foot, ankle, and hip joint distracted her from the conflict between sight and touch. She resisted it initially, just as she'd resisted the warmth of the grotto bath. Physical pleasure just led to physical pain when she over-reached the capabilities of her palsied limb. *I won't.*

"'Tis thy future, beloved."

Oh. She drew in a deep breath, released it. *I will.*

And she did.

With her surrender, the tingling grew stronger. She tensed again, and the sensation edged over into pain. She gasped. Immediately the pins-and-needles softened to the easier tickling.

"Stronger heals best. Canst bear it, dear heart?"

"I'll try, but –" Could she? It was hard to welcome . . . not discomfort really, but intensity.

"Be soft."

Yes, staying loose was critical. Could she manage it? The tickle became a tingle became pins-and-needles, became a vibrating buzz. *I can do it!* I *can* bear this! I can *welcome* this!

It didn't go on for very long. They returned her to the pool and then the snow pack before the next short session of intensity. Water, wings, snow, water. Eat and drink. Water, wings, snow, water. Sometimes the sky was blue and cloud-swept for the outside visit; others, black and star-spangled. She might have grown bored – the healing was every bit as repetitious as weaving or spinning – except she'd never experienced anything like this before. With each repetition, she felt strength and health increasing in her once-palsied limb. And with each repetition, she embraced *being* – not resisting – a little bit more.

One day, they let her stand on her own feet. She felt . . . crooked. *Have I forgotten how to straighten?* Then she realized: this was a new kind of straight. *I don't have to pull with my left side muscles, stretch with my right ones. I'm straight . . . and tall . . . without effort.* She cried again. *I'm not lame anymore.*

It wasn't quite that simple. She had to learn all over again how to walk. First at the shallower edges of the pool with a pegasus on each side for support, later in the flattest part of the meadow. And there were exercises, leg lifts and toe presses and such, both in the water and out. She was eager for it all. Moving this new body of hers was . . . hard work . . . yet effortless, just like Nial loping easily down the slope from the branching hall to the lodge. *My body was made to do all this!* It amazed her.

Amidst the wonder, she knew one flash of unease. "This feels so good," she told friend-dancer. "How could I bear it, if I were injured again?"

The pegasus seemed to smile. "Loss always hurts. And loss after other losses . . . be more fearful. Thee knowest more. But . . . beautiful climber, thee also knowest the answer."

"I do?" Sarvet let the calmness that seemed to pool somewhere beneath all her new experiences flow through her thoughts. Yes, she did know. "Receiving a gift is dangerous, but barring out risk in fear . . . is the greater loss."

"Yes."

When Sarvet was running and jumping and tumbling in the meadow, the cloud strider approached her. "It is time. Art healed."

She knew it was true. She was whole and healthy. And suddenly eager to do . . . whatever she would do next. *I've had my adventure, but there are more awaiting me!*

She rinsed her clothing in the grotto pool and hung it to dry from jagged spurs in the rock walls. She packed her rucksack, noticing that the jerky pouch was empty and the hardtack down to three pieces. It *was* time to go. She dressed. Her thistle-silk under garments were as soft as the hides of the pegasi, but their touch all over her body felt strange. She'd grown used to nakedness.

She'd imagined hiking down the way by which she'd come, but the pegasi had other ideas. "The blizzards of late winter lingered in the upper reaches. Thee wouldst require skis, intrepid walker!" Wind-caller whickered gently. "And . . . we should enjoy thy company a small time more."

Her flight home was magnificent. The cloud strider bore her. His back was solid and safe, as usual, but the entire world stretched out below them, a vast tapestry of snowy ranges, green valleys, and the far-off blue lowlands reaching to the line of the horizon. The pegasi climbed higher at first. Sarvet caught a glimpse of a small, brownish dot mid-slope on a neighboring mountain. "There!" And then they wheeled and spiraled down, down and down.

They landed in a clearing in the pine grove above the branching-hall, and Sarvet leapt to the ground. Now that the moment of parting had arrived . . . she didn't want to. "Will I . . . ever see you again?"

"Shalt dwell in our hearts forever, splendid one," wind-caller told her.

"Then . . . this *is* goodbye?"

"Even at parting, true friends never part." Friend-dancer nosed her one last time.

Sarvet gathered the courage to say what she really meant. "I love you."

"And we, thee," answered the cloud rider. "But know this, brave climber: thee mayst visit us whenever thy heart knowest the time to be ripe. We wilt not always await thee in our meadow on the Maara-mount, but when we do, shalt welcome thee."

Their leap into the sky was like a lightning strike in reverse. The power of it made Sarvet wonder that their hoofs had not kicked a portal open to the crystal caverns that were said to lie in the Fiordhammars' roots. She watched the winged horses soar out over the valley, then turn and circle ever upward into endless blue. They were gone.

She looked down. A small spring was flowing from a shallow, rock-lined cavity. She laughed. No portal to the underworld, but . . . perhaps . . . a flow of healing water? She dabbled her fingers in it: warm.

The first Kaunis-sisters she saw were her friends, Brionne and Amara, leading Timbilio – the little goat kid born out of season in late Sombry – away from the milking byre. Had he escaped from the makeshift stall in the garden shed *again*? Whatever his fault, he was feeling frisky. Amara's clutch on his collar came loose as he bucked and twisted. Brionne's swipe for him missed and put her in prime position to receive Timbilio's whirling butt to her seat. She jolted to her hands and knees, cursing: "Shun it!" Amara was no help, collapsing in giggles.

Sarvet stepped briskly forward, capturing the escapee as he attempted to dash past her with a well-timed grab for his ear. The goat grew docile under this persuasion, and she led him away from the branching-hall steps. Amara finally stopped laughing and looked up. Brionne stopped cursing and looked up. Both girls' mouths dropped open.

Brionne was the first to recover. "Sarvet!" she shrieked, leaping to her feet and hurtling into Sarvet's arms. "You're alive, you're back, you're tall! Oh, Sarvet, oh, Sarvet!" Then she burst into tears.

Luckily Amara was more collected in her response, since Sarvet's grasp on Timbilio's ear slackened upon Brionne's tumultuous arrival. Amara secured the frolicking goat by his collar and remarked, "Nial was frantic, but I thought he was being silly."

Brionne lifted her red face out of Sarvet's shoulder long enough to retort, "It might have been nothing that sent him looking, but he was right to be scared!

You know the tracks he found. Sarvet had fallen! And been hurt! She *crawled* back to the valley-rock. And then lost herself in the snowfall."

"I don't think so. I mean, look. She's fine. In fact . . ." Amara's voice trailed off. Apparently her preference for pretending the calmness of a grown sister failed under the unusual circumstance confronting her. And her indifference was certainly feigned. "Sarvet, what happened? You're . . . different!"

Sarvet smiled. "Come on! Let's get Timbilio here penned before he hustles you under the porch steps with his antics." Her friend was being jerked across the damp turf of the slope – the snow always melted here first – by the goat's jigging.

Amara's feigned composure cracked. "But you have to explain! Where've you been? Why did you go? *Were* you hurt? Tell us . . . oh, tell us everything!"

"Of course! But not –" This time she was the one stopping in mid sentence. What was Nial doing here? For it was unmistakeably Nial racing up the mountain from below the lodge. Surely the brothers of Tukeva-lodge had returned home – a month ago? or more? But it was Nial.

She awaited him, close to the spot where she'd awaited him before and with a similar intention, and yet how differently: she was full, not empty; she was confident, not desperate; and she would act openly, not in secret. Real strength had no need of secrecy.

"Sarvet! Sarvet!" Nial's embrace was more vigorous even than his mad dash upward. He lifted her off her feet, crushed her to him, spun around thrice, dabbed kisses all over her face, and then held her close, tenderly, as though she might break.

His chest felt good under her cheek, but she wanted to see his face. He let her go when she stepped back a bit. And his face was worth seeing: awe, love, and joy exalted his features. Was it truly for her return?

"I knew you were well!" he exclaimed. "More than well!" He looked her over in turn. "Sarvet, you're just the way I always saw you in my mind's eye . . . but never did see you in my fleshly eye. You're healed!"

She nodded.

"In more than your hip and foot."

She reached for his hand. "I'm healed in every way, Nial."

His excitement was moderating, mellowing into a steady joy much like her own.

Amara's laughter, happy rather than amused this time, broke the moment. And Timbilio jumped free. Again. Sarvet led the chase, just because she could, marveling at the way she too could now run all over this slope. It was exhilarating.

Once the goat was finally penned, she asked, "Will you come with me?"

Nial was too elated to be wary, but she could tell he thought twice before answering. He knew her well enough to suspect . . . something.

"I'd like you to hear what I will tell Mother Johtaia," she reassured him.

Someone must have caught sight of her through a lodge window – a few of the hide panels were off to let the warmish Nerich day inside – because Mother Johtaia evinced no surprise when the four of them crowded into her counsel-haven. Sister Kemra had kerin-tea and capricole savories ready, and four chairs arranged before the one in which the lodge-mother sat.

Johtaia arose, nodding to Amara, Brionne, and Nial, and took Sarvet's hands. Her smile was rueful. "I owe you an apology, Sarvet Kaunis-daughter."

Interesting. Sarvet tipped her head to one side. *I hadn't expected her to own it.*

"My solution wasn't . . . a solution. I take it you found a better one?"

Sarvet told her story. Nial had long since confessed its prelude: her determination to *take* a wanderyar – since one would not be given her – and his clandestine help. She gathered he'd felt misgivings within moments of her departure, resisted them for a while, then finally come after her. And been scared silly when he found evidence of her tumble and lost her tracks in the fresh snowfall. All the brothers of Tukeva-lodge had joined the Kaunis-sisters in searching through the night.

"I did fall," she confirmed. "And I did make it all the way back to the valley-rock. But . . . I couldn't bear to crawl back inside the husk I'd left behind."

Mother Johtaia nodded. Amara wrinkled her brows in puzzlement. Brionne and Nial looked guilty. Surely they didn't imagine her difficulties were *their* fault? Or maybe they did. It was easy to imagine you could have done more for a friend in need. Especially when looking back. It was usually more confusing at the time.

"I found *pegasi* on the mountain top. Pegasi!" she told them.

Nial's and Brionne's mouths dropped open. Mother Johtaia looked . . . wistful? Was it possible . . . she'd had her own experience with winged horses? There was knowingness to the far-off look in her eyes. Only Amara exclaimed, "No! There are no such! Not really." But Amara's disbelief faded as Sarvet continued her tale. She found it hard to describe her inner experiences. The outer events were easier to relate: the warm water, the snow packs, the labor of the exercises.

"It sounds awful!" sympathized Amara. "You poor thing! Were you very lonely and bored?"

Lonely! She'd never been so companioned in her life. *I must be doing a more wretched job of telling this than I thought. Amara doesn't get it at all!* But Johtaia looked as if she understood. And Nial's and Brionne's faces reflected wonder.

The lodge-mother didn't leave them long for contemplation of Sarvet's adventure. It was, after all, her job to be practical. "I'm glad it ended well, Sarvet. You do know it might not have."

Oh, yes. Sarvet nodded soberly. She would not have made it back down the mountain, if the pegasi had not been present to succor her at its top.

"Father Biejan and I have been talking these four sevendays."

"Are the Tukeva-fathers still here?" So that's why Nial was not long gone home.

"No. Nial's been tenting on their campsite alone." Mother Johtaia smiled wryly. "Biejan forbore to order, and I . . . well, I hadn't the heart to persuade."

Nial blushed.

"But Biejan agrees with me that some girls need a wanderyar as much or more than any boy." Johtaia paused. "You were right, Sarvet. And I was wrong."

"You mean Sarvet gets to have *more* adventures?" burst out Amara. Apparently she'd forgotten her earlier judgement of Sarvet's enterprise as boring and lonely. "That's not fair! I think she should be punished, not rewarded!"

Johtaia cast Amara a reproving glance, then continued with her own agenda. "But a girl embarking on a wanderyar needs *training* for it, as I think you have proved. In future, candidates will attend the ramble-class in Tukeva-lodge *before* they travel." Johtaia turned her gaze on Amara a moment. "That does include you, Amara, if you truly wish for adventure. Such undertakings *are* frequently uncomfortable." Then the lodge-mother's attention was back on Sarvet. "If you still desire a wanderyar, it is yours."

Sarvet laughed. When you weren't ready, things could be so difficult. And when you were . . . barriers folded like . . . Brionne going down at Timbilio's buffet. "I hadn't planned on asking you this time. I was just going to *tell* you. But yes, I am going."

Johtaia's laugh mirrored Sarvet's: delight and confidence at its heart. "*After* the ramble-class, I trust."

Sarvet grew serious. "I'd like the ramble-class, but may I join the one now in progress? I'm not waiting until you manage to organize a girls' class."

Johtaia was taken aback. Then she laughed again and shook her head. "I'm never quite prepared for you, am I, Sarvet?" She sighed. "Well, I needn't make the same mistake twice. If Biejan approves it, then you have my consent as well."

Amara groaned – a muted groan – and Brionne gasped. Even Sarvet herself wondered if maybe she'd been a bit *too* bold. *Where will I sleep in Tukeva-lodge?* Surely they wouldn't put her in a bednook in the boys' sleep-hall.

Nial was ahead of them. "My lodge-father has already cleared the callers' spare box-room for Sarvet's use. And moved one of the portable nooks into it. She can come to us today." His gaze, warm and proud, turned to Sarvet. "If it please you!"

"I'd like that!" Indeed, she'd hoped to depart today. Even after a month of intense change, she still felt . . . allergic to Kaunis-lodge. She wanted to sleep somewhere else.

Mother Johtaia moved swiftly to necessities. "You'd better pack another satchel, child." Her gaze sized up Sarvet's rucksack. "You'll want more than the clothes you stand up in." She hesitated. "I'll tell Paiam, if you like, but . . ."

Sarvet overrode this. "No, I can do it." Her voice sounded quiet, but firm in her ears. "I want to do it."

"Would you like me to come with you?"

"Yes, but . . . for her. Not me. I think –" Sarvet wasn't sure what her intuition was telling her, but she suspected Paiam needed . . . something. At least her birth-mother wouldn't be able to hide this further grief caused by her daughter. And she might try, if there were no witnesses. But just one. "Amara, Brionne . . . Nial –"

Nial understood before she requested or explained. "It's a private moment."

Johtaia nodded. "I feel sure you girls have a few chores still waiting . . ." Brionne nodded, conscience-stricken, and scrambled up to go finish her lodge tasks. Amara went with her, reluctantly. "Nial, you may make yourself comfortable here, if you wish."

Sarvet and Johtaia found Paiam at the small spinning wheel in her sitting room. Sarvet could see her birth-mother clamping down on her immediate impulse to leap from her seat. Paiam's jaw clenched. "So! You're not dead in a blizzard."

Johtaia was taken aback once more. *What is it about me and my mother?* Sarvet felt unsurprised. Paiam had been fighting her vulnerabilities for so long, she'd likely forgotten how to feel relief.

"I'm healed . . . Mother."

"At what cost?" grated Paiam.

Sarvet remembered wind-caller's words. "I've given up all my defenses, faced my worst fears, and let go of who I was."

"Then you're not my daughter." Paiam's voice was harsh. "I wouldn't have you, if you begged me."

Johtaia's consternation ripened to shock. "Sister! Think what you're saying!"

"I'm leaving, Mother." Sarvet felt sad, but not for herself. *If only my healing might have salved Paiam's wounds as well.* But each person had, apparently, to work out her own salvation.

"Did you think I didn't know?" Where Paiam's eyes the least bit shiny? Her teeth gripped her lip in anger.

"I wanted to say farewell, Mother."

"Well, you've said it." Paiam started her spinning wheel again.

"I love you."

Paiam opened her lips, shut them, and shook her head. "Long partings never prosper. Go."

Sarvet turned in the doorway and walked away. After a dismayed moment, Johtaia followed her.

"I *am* sorry, Sarvet. If I'd realized . . . well, I think I should have told her myself."

Sarvet smiled. "No. I knew how it would be. And I wanted to do it."

Her parting from her friends was more satisfactory. Amara gave her a small bound sheaf of pages and a stylus. "Write it all down, Sarvet," she urged. "I don't think I'm brave enough to go on a wanderyar! The only one I'll have will be by imagining yours. I want to hear *everything*!"

Brionne clung to her in an anxious hug. "Promise you'll come back, Sarvet," she whispered. "I know it's exciting out there, but . . . please come back."

"This is home," Sarvet reassured her. "And I'll be ready for home . . . after a year . . . or two . . . or three!"

"Oh, Sarvet! Three years?"

"Maybe. But not four, I promise. I want a wanderyar, not a new lodge-family. I'm Hammarleeding," she declared. And she was. But this wanderyar felt . . . essential.

The ramble-class would be the beginning. What Hammar-sister had ever guested in a father-lodge before? Except, really, her wanderyar began with the inner journey in the sanctuary of the pegasi. And would never end – despite her promise to Brionne – even when she returned home. She did intend to return home, to Kaunis-lodge. *I'll be traveling through time, through life, through the great adventure of being. And that never needs to stop.* Is that what Nial learned on his wanderyar?

Nial, of course, went with her on this first leg of the journey. He *was* going home.

hree years later, Sarvet strode along the Ulko-polku, arms swinging and shoulders loose. She'd lightened her pack at the Tukeva-sawmill; no need to bring camping gear and coin back to Kaunis-lodge. The brothers would see that the next wanderleeding out got them. She drew a deep breath in through her nose: the mystic scent of the pines mingled with warmer aromas of risa-turf and starflowers. She'd not yet reached the familiar landmarks of the Vrea-vale, cradled by Maara-mount and Valtava-scarp and the Tunkahorn, but the alpine valleys and their towering snow-capped peaks were all around her. *I'm home!* And she was ready to be home. The world was a fascinating, enthralling place, but . . . she craved the pleasures of staying put now. And the place where she wanted to settle was at her origin. She knew some wanderleedings *didn't* come home. But for Sarvet, her birthplace in the Fiordhammars was the right spot.

What will I tell them, once I'm home? There was so much! She'd travelled south. Nial's adventures beckoned her fancy, but her heart whispered of making her own discoveries, and she'd not traced his steps after all. Amara would hate the first bit on the fishing boat. Sarvet glanced down at her right wrist. The scar from the spinefish would likely fade over the years, but never entirely disappear. But she'd loved the waves and the salt breeze and the energy of the sailors and fishers. Once her stomach got used to the constant surge of the water.

Brionne would like the lady-chapels of Fiorish. But that tale wouldn't do for the first burst of news and greeting. The sweet healing of the baby born with the malkin-lip needed a more private telling. And she wasn't sure she could share the other miracles she'd witnessed in those sacred spaces. *I wouldn't have believed my own eyes, if I hadn't experienced my own miracle on the Maara-mount.*

And her visit with her father – Ivvar – at Rakas-lodge, was too intimate, too lovely and special, to share at all.

But she could certainly talk about the many cowherds of Erice, as well as the spiceflower fields on that island. The rose plantations of Frisange and Sarvet's work in the distillery where the rose-attar was made would interest Sister Evaia, although her apprenticeship to the antiphoner in Imsterfeldt would be the biggest draw for the healer. Odd how Sarvet's earlier experiences in her wanderyar – Merovessic fish, miracles on the Isle of Fiorish, spiceflowers, and rose-attar – had fitted her perfectly for Maittresse Saussen's purposes.

But what would she tell Nial? Everything. *When would she tell Nial? Maybe I'll turn right instead of left at the Vrea-way and go straight to Tukeva-lodge.* She'd been missing Nial with an almost physical ache for the past half year. But when she reached the path toward home she turned left. She wanted to test herself in her native milieu. *Have I truly grown enough to face Paiam?* Her birth-mother seemed a small figure in her memory after three years away. Would she loom larger in Kaunis-lodge? *I hope not. I want to settle there, and I can't do it, if I can't keep my own perspective in Paiam's presence.* But she felt strong. *I'm ready. I know I am.*

Around the bulk of the valley-rock, a surprising sight met her gaze. The father-camp was filled with a flock of tents, along with milling men and boys. What were the Tukeva-brothers doing here now?

Then she caught a glimpse of one Tukeva-brother in particular, at the same time he saw her.

"Nial!"

"Sarvet!"

She didn't await him this time. Nor did he await her. She shed her rucksack just before she stepped into his arms.

"Sarvet, lovely Sarvet, oh, Sarvet," he murmured, folding her close and kissing her hair. He was still the taller. He'd shot upwards more while she was away; but she'd grown too. She lifted her face.

His lips were warm, urgent. A delicious tingling – it had scared her when she was fifteen – rose through her body. Her own lips parted. *Nial, oh, Nial!*

She'd never received the linking-lessons from Sister Kilti, but Maittresse Saussen had discovered her ignorance and pressed several informative Cambers-scrolls upon her. She stopped her fingers from from opening Nial's sweater toggles with an effort. *We can't celebrate an adoration right here on the edge of the father-camp!*

Nial released her, panting. His eyes were bright and dark. "Do you know what day it is?"

She shook her head, wondering.

"It's the skip-span, and Other-joy is late this year."

So that's why the fathers are here!

"Sarvet" – Nial knelt before her, taking her hands in his – "Will you commune with me?" His eyes held something more than love. It was a pledge . . . like the one that Cambers men and women made to one another . . . but that wasn't part of Hammarleeding culture. Nial wanted to adore her forever. And she –?

Sarvet knelt in turn and pressed his fingers. "Always," she breathed. "This Other-joy and the next and the next. Until our very last."

He kissed her palms. She nipped his thumb.

And they both joined the father-procession when it started up the hill for Kaunis-lodge. *Poor Johtaia,* thought Sarvet irrelevantly, *she'll be just as shocked by my method of homecoming as she was by my wish to leave in the first place.* She smiled at Nial smiling back at her.

On the lodge-porch, Sarvet accepted symbolic pannkuja from an astonished Sister Unni. *If I'm going to be a tradition-breaker, I may as well break them thoroughly,* she decided. Besides, she was hungry.

Johtaia had not yet seen Sarvet in the crowd. The lodge-mother began the presentations of the sister-novitiates to the brother-novices. This year there were five couples, and one of those were Brionne and Vaino. Vaino knelt and kissed Brionne's hands. Brionne flushed. She looked happy and starry-eyed.

Sarvet stepped forward with Nial for the lodge-mother's blessing. Mother Johtaia's face registered just the surprise Sarvet was expecting. Then she laughed and shook her head. "Welcome home, Sarvet!" And she really meant it. But couldn't forebear remarking: "I suppose a quiet return on an ordinary day would never have been right for you!" Leaving her formal role aside for a moment, she moved to embrace her prodigal daughter and kissed Sarvet on the cheek. Her voice grew wry. "I take it you wish to celebrate a linking with Nial?"

"Yes, I do."

Johtaia smiled, nodded, and returned to the ritual words. "Sisters of Kaunis and brothers of Tukeva, I call on you to search your hearts. Two of our body have discovered without sanction their desire to share a linking-moon. Is there a brother who will speak for Nial Ilggai-spring and his descent lines? Is he fit to adore a woman?"

Father Biejan came forward. "I speak for him."

"It is well," Johtaia intoned. "Is there a sister who will speak for Sarvet Paiam-spring and her decent lines? Is she fit to be adored?"

Sarvet held her breath. *Would* anyone speak for her? It had to be a once-linked (or more) sister who knew Sarvet's genealogy. She searched the congregation of women clustered on the porch. Where were the green-sister and the byre-sister? Surely they would speak for her. But no one was moving forward.

Several of the sisters near the front portal shifted; three moved aside. The long silence hung. Then Sarvet's birth-mother stepped forth.

She looked different. What was this difference? Her clothes were the same drab sepia Paiam had worn for years. She was just as tall and angular as always. And her face was serious. But not . . . tense. Was that peace in her expression?

Paiam's gaze met Sarvet's and . . . softened? She smiled, a slow smile that reached all the way to her eyes and beyond. She walked to Johtaia's side, claiming the traditional honor for a novitiate's birth-mother. "*I* speak for Sarvet. She is beautiful and whole. She is fully fit to be adored . . . *and to adore!*" All through her declaration Paiam gazed with love and pride upon her child, now grown to womanhood.

Sarvet's eyes grew damp and her vision blurred. *She's healed . . . and free of some darkness that's ridden her ever since my birth.* Paiam's heart was whole.

THE END